COLD RETRIBUTION

Cold Vengeance
Book 3

NOLON KING

DAVID W. WRIGHT

STERLING & STONE

To YOU, the reader.
Thank you for your support.
Thank you for the wonderful emails.
Thank you for the thoughtful reviews.
Thank you for reading and loving our stories.

Chapter One

Stan felt like a father at the end of his rope. Trying to keep his family happy on a long trip home after a stressful vacation.

The drive through the night to the Belling airport had been a slow one. Taking it easy against the certainty that somebody was already there waiting for them.

Each of them had taken their turn in the tiny shower. He was last, barely enough water was left, but when he finished, he felt like he could take the first deep breath of the day.

Jeans and t-shirt. A clean sock for his left foot. A nice cleanup of the Everyday Carry before slipping his stump into the socket and pumping it down.

Gen insisted on helping him so she could inspect the skin. "I don't need a nurse," he snapped.

"Maybe not, but I'm still looking."

As short as she was, she still seemed to fill up the remaining space in the van, so he let her push him down onto the bed. "Fine. Look all you want."

Ronnie ignored him. Probably punishment for leaving her sitting in the mud.

He wasn't even sure why he did it. Imagining the world without her had made it seem like she was already gone.

When Gen was done, he didn't bother trying to get to a seat. He sat on the bed instead, looking at the last bit of luxury he'd see for a while.

It had been his plan to use this van for a long time. Now they were going to leave it at the airport. Maybe they could come back and get it when this was all done. Use it when they had to get back on the run.

Mo pulled into the long-term lot just as the sun brightened the edge of the sky. Pulled in next to a tiny smart car. They all climbed out, weary and bleary-eyed.

He and Mo carried the bags. A few days' worth of essentials. He would have to rely on Ian for anything more. Reminded himself to keep his phone charged so he wouldn't miss the call.

The inside of the airport shuttle was silent on the two-mile drive to the passenger drop-off. Gen and Ronnie sat side by side, leaning together with their heads touching. Mo stood up the whole way, holding on to a ceiling strap and staring at the back of the driver's head.

They shuffled out into the bright lights in front of the entrance. Ronnie and Gen went inside to the Hill of Beans that was piping the burnt smell of coffee into every corner.

He used the app to get a FASTr. Asked for something with room. They'd still probably send a Civic.

He sat on the metal bench next to the ashtray and leaned his head back on the window. When he closed his eyes, he saw Frank. It felt like a memory from a decade ago, but he knew it was just before things changed. Sitting at his dining room table eating that horrible chicken Marsala he couldn't stop making.

Frank told him about the little girl across the street. Her father was raping her, and she had asked Frank to kill him. He told her he would help, but only to get him arrested, not to kill him.

Stan had seen the lie in the way Frank worried his hands into fists. The set of his shoulders. He would catch that man, and he would kill him.

Stan had secretly approved.

He felt a touch in his hand. Bolted upright in surprise to find Ronnie sliding a cup of coffee into his fingers. Before walking away, she took a moment to caress the back of his hand, up to his wrist. She didn't look at him, but she nodded before turning away to sit with Gen again.

Mo stayed on his feet, leaning his hip against a concrete post.

FASTr surprised Stan with a Chrysler Town & Country. More than enough room for them all to sit along with the driver — a chatty housewife working her van at the airport to make extra money for a new wheelchair for her disabled husband.

She took them to a park ten miles outside of town. Dropped them off next to a large gazebo.

Stan paid cash. Included an extra twenty, and the driver gasped in pleasure. Put her hand on her heart. "Thank you so much." It looked like she was about to cry. "I hope you have a blessed day."

"You too." He watched her disappear into a cloud of gravel dust. Turned to see Gen sitting with her back against a stone wall. Ronnie's head in her lap. Opal finger twining through the broad curls of her hair.

Mo bent in front of a small grill on top of a pole set into concrete. Adjusting the height of the grates. Nodding in satisfaction.

When his phone vibrated, he realized he had been

standing there in the rising sun for several minutes. He fished it out of his pocket. "Yeah."

"We should be in town by 3:30."

"Copy that."

"Any additional requirements?"

Stan told him he might need to work as a handler for a time. Get them a motel room. Some food. Go from there.

"Check."

"I'll send our location, and then it's just waiting, waiting."

"Half the world is waiting."

Ian hung up, and Stan sighed his agreement.

He turned the GPS on. Took a picture of the peak of the gazebo. Turned the GPS back off. Now the picture was tagged with his location. He emailed it to Ian's secure mail server.

Waited for the ping of a return email, confirmation that Ian had received the message.

Nothing to do but wait seven hours.

Mo was on the ground next to Gen. They all seemed asleep. Mo had his feet up on the bags. Another one under his outstretched hand.

Stan didn't want to disturb them so he climbed onto a creaking picnic table. Let his Everyday Carry dangle over to rest on the seat as he lay back. Folded his hands over his belly and fell asleep.

He woke up with the sound of a hissing alligator echoing in his mind. His missing foot ached. His head throbbed. It felt like he had a pound of sand in his sinuses.

He sat up with a groan. The luggage was by the wall, but Mo and the girls were gone.

He looked around and found Ronnie standing in front of a row of vending machines. Stan didn't remember seeing them before his nap.

Gen and Mo were by a water fountain, splashing their legs and arms.

None of them looked like they were on a cookout.

He stood for a stretch. Heard the crunch of gravel as a small SUV — a Honda of some kind — approached followed by a white van.

Mohammed was behind the wheel of the Honda. Ian in his place driving the van. Mo met him at the front of the SUV with a bottle of Coke. Stan killed half of it while Mohammed and Ian got out.

Mohammed tossed the keys to Ian and climbed into the side door of the van. Ian tossed the keys to Stan.

"I got you a room at a motel down the road. East out of the main entrance here. Two miles down, the Night Post. Shawna made a quick trip to Provisions for food. We don't have a list of allergies or preferences, so there's just a variety."

Stan nodded. "I'm sure it'll be fine."

Ian sighed. "There's also a competitor in the area."

"What, another Household Services contractor?"

"Yeah. We knocked the logo off the van here. Gonna put a rack and some wire on it. Use a phone company livery for a while. Then we'll sniff 'em out. That's how they knew where you were going. It wouldn't take much to extrapolate using the kind of gear they have access to. But they're hindered by the office. I am not so hindered."

Stan sighed. Things were about to get more difficult and more expensive. "So what now?"

Ian pointed at the gazebo. "This was smart. I'm almost positive you're good right now. I know we are." He tipped his head at the keys in Stan's hand. "The room keys are on that ring. Go and rest up for a bit. Let us scour around, then we'll meet up later for some planning."

Without waiting for confirmation, he turned and went

back to the van. Stan didn't watch him leave. Instead he turned to Mo. "Did we do the right thing?"

Mo shrugged. "We did the only thing."

That's what Stan had been afraid of. If there was only one thing, there were no more choices.

Chapter Two

Jeanette only felt safe when she was touching him. Like contact with him bled strength into her. But the dependency made her feel weak.

The way the men had tried to hurt her had been terrifying. The way Haggis had reacted had been almost as scary. But he had handled her so gently afterward. Helping her clean up, never rushing her when she broke down.

She cursed herself because she always thought she was stronger than that.

They shuffled through the aftermath, ignored the ringing phone, and slept in a shared embrace.

The smell of fresh coffee woke her up. Only one eye working. The split in her left eyebrow felt like a throbbing water balloon.

Haggis stood there in the strip of morning sunlight coming through the curtains, sipping at a cup. His back was oddly hairless considering the red fur that nearly covered the rest of him. Except for a small diamond of fluff in the hollow of his lumbar spine.

He looked soft but powerful. Even bigger without his shirt on.

The bodies of the men that had attacked her were gone. She couldn't figure out where he had put them or how she had slept through him doing it.

A small pile of what they had carried was a jumble on the table next to the hutch that held the bar and TV. Guns and holsters. A wad of cash. Some crumpled papers. What looked like a wrapped condom.

When she pulled the blanket back to roll toward the edge, the movement made her hesitate with a wince. She struggled to get her feet on the floor, remembered she was naked, and realized it didn't matter.

She stood with a groan. He turned to watch her walk, and she pushed her ratty hair back and held her hands out.

He held his cup up as she pushed into him. Gasped in shock at how cold the fronts of his thighs were. "You're freezing," she said. Her voice was a toad's croak.

He chuckled. "I was standing in front of the AC while the coffee brewed."

"Why?"

"That's where I put 'em. In between the bed and the window."

She nodded as she pushed away and headed for the bathroom. The floor felt like it had been swept. Since the room had no vacuum or broom, he must have gotten on his hands and knees with a towel or something. Just to be clean, or to protect her feet?

With the bathroom door closed behind her, she avoided anything more than a flash of her reflection. Brushed her teeth with her eyes closed. Brushed her hair by feel. Gritting her teeth with every tangle.

By the time she got dressed, her head was pounding. She took a bracing breath and finally looked.

Her left eye looked like a split apple. Waxy and red like at the grocery store. Her eyebrow was a crust of blackened blood. Skin turning purple up into her hairline.

Spreading down her cheek. A dark hollow under the other eye.

Tears squeezed through the swelling. Her face was scarred. Maybe she could get some tape on it, but there was no chance of going to a doctor. She was on the run now.

She squared her shoulders. Dabbed at the tears. Forced herself to look at it without flinching. Nodded to herself before marching out, her head giving a stab of pain with each step.

Haggis was dressed and leaning on the table with the coffee cup back in his hand. He pointed to the other cup next to him. "It's just black. I didn't know how you took it."

Smiling pulled at the scab, but she did it anyway. "Black's fine."

When he slid the cup over, his face fell into the light. Blackened eyes under a weeping gash on his forehead. Smaller cuts dotting the rest of his face.

"Oh," she said. Fighting fresh tears, she ignored the coffee to hug him again. The good side of her face against his flannel shirt. It smelled fresh.

She drew back. "Where did you get this?"

"I went out to my truck in your robe."

She laughed, then stilled her face at the pop of pain in her eyebrow. "You must have been hanging all out of it."

He grinned. "It was a little chilly."

She waved at the window. "When did you have time for all this?"

"Oh, I only sleep four or five hours a night. I'm good."

She sipped her coffee. Wished it had a little bourbon in it. "Now what?"

"I think we go to Texas."

"Why?"

He took a measuring breath. "I want to talk to Stan face-to-face. Any call might be intercepted, but I'll still have to find out where he went."

"To help him?"

He nodded. "Yes. I think what he's doing is worth supporting … and I'm pissed."

"Me too."

He smiled. "Maybe for different reasons."

She spread her hands. "What's more reason than this?"

He sat down. Fidgeted with the empty coffee cup. "I don't know how you did it, but you got me so tied up I can't even think straight."

The other chair had shattered on his face last night, so she took her cup to sit on the corner of the bed before her knees gave out. He didn't turn to face her.

"When I came in here and saw what they were doing," he said, looking up at the ceiling in thought, "it was like the pain they had done to you … that they were planning to do … it was like they were doing it to me. And I got so red. Like I couldn't believe they dared to do that to my girl."

He glanced over with a sheepish smile. "I knew you probably wouldn't like me calling you mine like that, but at that moment, it was all I could think, 'cuz hurting you was hurting me."

He looked back to his empty cup. "I don't know what right I have to think that. To want to protect you so much, but like I said … a guy is sitting here head over heels hopeless."

She stared at him spinning the cup in his hands. Stalling for time because she didn't know what to say. Even before Mark had left her — when she thought he still loved her — he had never said anything that made her feel as good about herself as what she had just heard.

"Then let's go to Texas," she said.

He nodded like she had just given him an order. "Sounds good."

He carried everything on the way out, and she let him. It meant she could hide her face against him. Keep his arm in her hands. Maintain that contact she suddenly craved.

She was sure they were on camera. There was nothing in her car she needed, so they walked all the way out to where Haggis had parked. The second row pointed toward the road. Ready to drive right out with just a flick of the wheel.

He put her stuff in the back under the hard bed cover. Walked her to the passenger side. Waited for her to get in and buckle up before closing the door.

His chivalry felt genuine. Like a habit born from treating women with respect for his entire life. If they were together twenty years from now, she was certain he would still wait for her, holding the door for as long as it took.

The old truck started without hesitation on the first twist. He bent to move the floor shifter into drive, but before he could pull out, she unbuckled and slid across the bench seat to the middle. Dug the middle belt out.

After she was buckled back in, he drove away.

She leaned against him. Put her hand on his thigh. It felt good, and he didn't seem to mind. When his big arm dropped across her shoulders, she closed her eyes.

What a bunch of bullshit to go through just to find somebody that made her feel good.

Chapter Three

Mo thought the room was far too small for all these people. Stan and his … family? Ian and his team. Spread out with crinkling fast food bags on the bed, the counter, balanced in laps.

Mo wasn't as big a fan of Sloppy's as Stan was, but he was hungry. Plus, it had been months since he had given a shit about his diet. He shrugged as he took another bite.

Seven people were eating on less than fifty bucks. Ah, America.

He looked up in surprise when Gen, Ronnie, and Shawna stood up at the same time. Ronnie held up her drink. "We girls are going into the other room. There are things we need to discuss."

Nobody objected, everyone sharing the same clueless look. When they opened the front door to leave, Ian nodded as he wiped his mouth. "Be cautious," he said.

His wistful look as they walked out made Mo wonder if something was going on between Ian and Shawna. He could understand. She was pretty enough, and plenty of people got romantic at work.

The ensuing silence was broken only by chewing and slurping. Wadding up wrappers and going in for more. When the meal slowed down toward the end, Ian said, "There's probably eyes on the bank."

Stan nodded. "Probably everywhere in town. Maybe even in this motel."

Ian smiled. "Not out here yet. But that doesn't mean they won't widen their search, or follow one of us here if we're not careful."

Mo dug out his last fry. "We'll just have to be careful then."

Ian leaned back. Put his drink between his legs. "You guys will have to scope out the bank. I don't mind being your gopher, but I am threatening my anonymity, which is fine as long as my price is being met … and I'm alive to spend it."

Stan stood up to walk to the window. "That's as much up to you as it is to me."

Ian smiled. "Agreed, but there are limits to what a service contractor like me can do when it comes to behavior in and around banks. That is something I am unwilling to tackle."

"Regardless of price?" Stan asked.

Ian spread his hands, and his smile became a grin. "Well …"

Mo knew Gen thought Ian was creepy, and Mo could see it. But it didn't stop him from liking the guy. He was good, and he knew it. And he backed it up with performance above and beyond any Household Services operative he had ever worked with.

Stan waved it away. "I can go right in anyway. They want me there."

Mo shook his head. "It's not the going in part, but the

getting back out alive part that you should be thinking about."

Stan pointed with the hand holding his cup. "Then think."

Mo held up one hand. "I did. We need a distraction. Something a couple blocks away that will draw eyes. Pull an official response."

Ian nodded as he leaned forward. "But only if we eliminate any threats already watching."

Mo shrugged. "If you can identify them."

"Oh, it will no doubt be the other Household Services contractor. I'll identify them all right. And then I'll fuck them."

Mohammed grinned. He had asked them all to call him Jihad, but Ian didn't use the nickname, and Mo thought it had been a joke. "Hard," he said. It was the first word Mo had heard him say, and he was surprised there was no accent. Then he felt guilty for thinking there should have been one.

"It's simple," Mo said. "We just have to get our eyes down there. Look at every nearby building. Every route of entry. What speedbumps there might be. Is a street fair coming to town? Is there a fucking hotdog vendor on the corner? Are any lanes closed?"

"Places to hide," Stan said. "Easy escape routes."

"Hard escape routes. *Any* escape routes."

Stan held up a finger. "Then, if we assume we are successful, we have to get the evidence to as many people as possible."

Ian and Mohammed exchanged a look. Ian nodded. "I think we can help with that. We got a server we've used for years to flood LiveLyfe with political misinformation. It's super effective. It eats up power and generates so much heat we have to reflow a lot of the solder when the boards separate, but it can hit a million plus users in a day. Couple that with the way shit is organically shared on the platform, and pretty soon, a hundred million people have seen it. If the news catches wind, who knows how many it will hit? Who can hide from that?"

"Something like that is terrifying," Mo said.

Ian nodded. "I know. It just costs so fucking much, even rich fucks don't see the value."

"Yeah, but they aren't trying to expose a pedophile ring."

Mohommed snorted laughter. "They're probably in on it."

"As expensive as it may be," Stan said, "I still need something more."

Ian shrugged. "A copy farm. Like a stack of flash drives. Fill 'em with the evidence and mail a thousand of 'em. Once the Livelyfe spam gets traction, that story will be money."

Stan shook his cup, but it was only ice. Looked at it with annoyance before dropping it in the trash can by the TV. "So all we have to do is get rid of anybody who might be staking the bank out while avoiding anybody that might be looking for us. Get into a bank that probably has somebody in there waiting for us. Get back out after opening my safety deposit boxes —"

"Boxes?" Mo said.

Stan tipped his head in a little shrug. "One is evidence, the other is money."

"Do you know which is which?"

Ian leaned forward. "That's right, make sure you get the right one."

Stan chuckled. "I'm sure we all know which one you would rather I save."

Ian sat up straight like he'd been slapped. "The one with the evidence. The one that will save those girls. Jesus."

Stan sighed. "I'm sorry. I just … "

Ian held his hand up. "I get it. I talk about getting paid often enough. It's easy to believe it's all I think about. So make sure you get the right one."

"Roger that."

Ian grinned. "I mean, I'll still bill you."

When Stan burst out laughing, Mo sat forward to put his elbows on his knees. "This is all very heartwarming, but we still haven't gotten to the part where we need to get away, and then stay away after this shit comes to light. Do we need more support?"

A buzzing phone sank the room into silence. It was Stan's. After studying the screen, his eyes widened as he answered. "Yeah."

Mo couldn't hear the other voice. He watched Stan's face as he closed his eyes. Shoulders sagging.

"Got it," Stan said. "I'll call back soon."

He sighed as he dropped the phone back into his pocket. Scrubbed his face with both hands and looked at Mo. "That was Haggis."

Ian held up one hand. "That damn grizzly that works for you?"

Stan nodded. "Jeanette Gustoff's with him. Gen was right. A couple guys from the office traced 'em to the room I got for her."

Ian nodded. "They definitely have a contractor helping them. It had to be after we left."

"It was."

"What happened?" Mo asked.

"He killed them."

Mo clapped his hands. "My man!"

Ian looked from Mo to Stan. "He an operator?"

Stan shrugged. "Marine Corps sniper."

"And he's an ox, so I can see it."

Mo felt a little better about their chances. "Looks like we got that support I was asking for."

Stan walked to the front door. "What's that gonna cost though?"

He walked out. Pulled the door shut with barely a click.

Mo didn't think he was talking about money.

Chapter Four

It had been easy for Ronnie to convince Gen to go next door. Shawna had taken a little more convincing. When Ronnie had pointed out how they were being ignored anyway, it had made her case a little easier.

They arranged themselves at the small table that looked like it had been cleaned with sandpaper. Gen pulled out a surprise bottle of wine. Shawna said she couldn't possibly, but then caved so fast, they all ended up laughing.

It was a good start.

Then Gen asked why she didn't want to stay to listen to the plan. "Haven't we both been bitching nonstop about being left out? About how we are more than charms on a bracelet?"

"Ooh, that's good," Shawna said.

Instead of answering, Ronnie pointed at Shawna's plate. "Who gets a salad from Sloppy's?"

She shrugged. "I used to be … bigger."

Gen finally looked away from Ronnie to address Shawna. "How much?"

Shawna looked down at her lap. "Quite a bit."

She had a pretty accent. Not quite southern. "What happened?"

Shawna smiled, but it was twitchy and nervous. Ronnie reached across the table. "Never mind. It doesn't matter."

Shawna sighed in relief.

Gen nodded. "Yeah, sorry. I was just curious. You're cute as shit anyway."

What a peculiar way to say it. Ronnie wondered if she had already been drinking. Saw the way the muscles in her jaw bulged. The way her knuckles stood out as she held the bottle.

She was pissed. Before Ronnie could ask herself what she was mad about, she realized. Gen was mad at her.

Instead of addressing it, she focused her attention back on Shawna. "You know ... Ian has the hots for you."

She turned so red, Ronnie thought she was holding her breath. "I don't think so," she gasped.

Gen tipped her head to the side. "I always thought he was ... creepy."

Shawna's eyes widened. "Oh no. I can see how somebody might think that, but he's just very intense. In fact, I've never seen him so relaxed."

Gen leaned back. "He does seem different than the last time I worked with him."

Shawna nodded. "With Mr. Grimm."

"That's right."

Shawna shrugged as she took another nibbling bite. "He likes Stan a lot."

Ronnie took a drink of wine. It was from a Styrofoam cup, but it was still tasty. "Stan's easy to like. Hard to love."

"I think Ronnie's right," Gen said. "Ian is into you."

Shawna put her fork down and folded her hands in her lap. "I used to work for the CIA. A long story for a long time ago. I fell in love with the man I was handling. Do you know what that means?"

Ronnie shook her head right as Gen nodded. "A bad guy you were working," she said.

Shawna nodded and looked back down. "Like one of those women that marries a prisoner or sends letters to Charles Manson. And I did love him. I remember it."

She paused for another bite of salad. Crunched on a crouton. Took a drink. Ronnie was fascinated by the precision of her movements.

"It was a relationship that ended my career, and I was very good at my job … right up until I met Miguel. He was a feeder. Do you know what that is?"

This time Gen shook her head as Ronnie nodded. "A man who gets off on watching a woman eat."

"Oh," Gen whispered.

"It was years," Shawna said. "And he posted videos. And I let him. And it went on and on. And then one day, he introduced me to another man, one that wanted a person good with computers, one that was easily controlled. I was so big, I couldn't move well."

A tear rolled down her cheek. She took another bite, and her lips curled as if she was disgusted by the texture. "And I went to work for this man. I created a network that nobody could get into. One so tight, even the contractors from Household Services couldn't get in."

Gen leaned forward in awe. "You beat Ian?"

Shawna nodded, and another tear came down. "But Miguel no longer fed me. No longer touched me. Just came around to call me a worthless fat bitch."

She looked away. Tears flowed. "I wanted to die, but they had me chained to my terminal with my obesity. I started to insert holes in the network. Stopped eating every single bite they shoved in front of me. Standing up from my chair was a struggle. Left me breathless after just one, but I kept going. Then Ian found one of the holes I left, and he knew … he knew I had done it on purpose."

She smiled and wiped her cheeks dry. Turned back for another bite, but left it on the fork, hanging in the air on the way to her mouth. "The day they raided us, Miguel came in with a knife, demanding what I had done. But he was used to the woman I had been. I told him exactly what was coming, and when he attacked me, I pulled the knife I had taken from the cheese tray. Just a little thing. But where his knife stabbed into a layer of fat, mine went right through his ribs."

She finally took the bite. Put the fork down to dab at her mouth with a red, white, and blue napkin. "Ian found me with Miguel on top of me, bleeding to death in my lap, his knife sticking out of my fat roll. And he grabbed Miguel by the back of the neck. Dragged him off like he was a bag of trash. Like he was uncovering something that was actually worth something by wiping the grime away. And he told me my work was the best he'd ever seen. And he told me somebody as pretty as me shouldn't be locked up in the dark …"

Her face collapsed at the memory, and she buried her face in her hands. "And he gave me my job back. My life back." Then she shook her head. "But he doesn't want me. He's never ever said anything. I'm too fat. All this loose skin. Who would want me?"

She took a deep breath and wiped her face with the Sloppy's napkin. Smoothed her brown uniform shirt down. "No, I don't think he has the hots for me."

Gen sat with both hands over her mouth. Tears glistening. Ronnie leaned forward to put her hand on Shawna's arm. "But what about you?"

She shook her head. "Me what?"

"How do you feel about him?"

Her face lit with joy. Ronnie was sure if Ian could see it, he would ask her to marry him. "I love him," Shawna said.

Gen lunged forward. "Then tell him."

Shawna shook her head. "No. I couldn't."

"You have to."

"I don't think so."

"Shawna – "

She slammed her hand onto the table. Chest heaving. "I said no!"

Ronnie jumped back, but Gen wouldn't be denied. She took Shawna's other hand, and Ronnie knew there was no way she could pull away. "If you ever had a thing to do, ever a regret to avoid, this is the one. Sweety, don't close the door at least."

Shawna closed her eyes, but her other hand crept out to cover Gen's. "Okay. Just … not now."

Ronnie gasped in shock. "You'll tell him?"

She shrugged as Gen let her hand go. "Yes. Soon."

Gen turned to Ronnie. "And what about you?"

She acted like she didn't know what Gen was talking about. "But I don't love Ian."

Gen smacked her lips like she had tasted something stale. "That's not what I'm talking about. Why excuse yourself all the sudden?"

Ronnie shrugged. "You know, girl talk."

"Bullshit. What are you doing?"

Ronnie picked at the hair hanging in her face. "I'm giving him what he wants."

Gen spread her hands. "He wants you."

"I don't blame him," Shawna said. "You're gorgeous."

Ronnie looked down to hide her face. "I'm not."

Shawna laughed. "I was in incredible shape when I

23

first started with the CIA, and I wasn't close to having a body like yours."

"Yeah, but did you have a face like mine?"

Gen rolled her eyes. "Amazing how we're the only ones that see the flaws, huh?"

Ronnie pulled more of her hair down to obscure her face. "You would know."

"Yes, I would know. And you still haven't answered me."

Shawna reached out and touched Gen's braid. "But that's so beautiful."

Gen nodded. "I think so, but except for taking care of it, it's just a part of me. Like the color of my eyes. Something I can't control. That's what Ronnie doesn't get. Her face isn't her fault. I did this to myself. I made myself into a freak."

Ronnie shook her head. "Yet you still found love."

"So did you."

"So did I," Shawna said. "Everybody has their thing."

Gen's face opened in shock. Then she burst out laughing. "You got me." She pointed at Ronnie. "But I still want to hear what's going on over there."

Ronnie sighed. "I told you. He needs me out of the way, so I'm staying out of the way."

"That doesn't make any sense."

"If I can keep him focused, he might make it through this. If that happens, little girls get saved. How hard is that to understand?"

Gen held her palms up in confusion. "Do more by doing nothing?"

"That's right."

Gen sneered. "Well, I'm not doing it.'

"That's your choice."

Gen stood. Drained her Styrofoam cup. Took the

bottle as she walked away, slammed the door on her way out.

Shawna put the cover back on her salad. "I think she's right. I learned a long time ago that fighting was worth it. I'd rather die trying to be better than live knowing I could have been."

She didn't slam the door when she left, but Ronnie still flinched when it closed.

Chapter Five

Haggis knew where Stan was going. The bank in Belling, Texas. He and Jeanette had pieced a lot together. Like they had one of those friendship lockets. Tidbits of Stan's story in his, a few more in hers, all meshed together to make a bigger picture.

While driving into town, he saw plenty of Chevy square bodies. Old trucks in various states of disrepair and restoration. And fellas that looked like him were a dime a dozen down here.

He wasn't too worried about being identified, and Jeanette's face had taken on the color of burning dusk. Her own mother would have passed her on the street.

She was afraid she wouldn't heal the same. He resisted the urge to tell her it didn't matter to him what she looked like. That's not what she wanted to hear. "The body is strong, Grasshopper," he said. "It knows how to repair itself."

That had seemed to satisfy her.

He found a motel coming into town. Across the highway from one that looked like its sheets might be slightly cleaner. The one he picked had only one floor. A pool with a soda machine next to it. Classy.

When he got his key, he opened Jeanette's door, and she leaned on his arm as she got out. He bet her head was a jackhammer. His wasn't too smooth, but he could tolerate it. His anger was keeping him on his feet.

He led her to the bed. Eased her down, and she curled up on her good side. He told her he was going to get some food. Check out the bank.

"Which bank?"

"I'll Google it. How many can there be in this town? Don't answer the door for anything."

She was already asleep.

It turned out there were four banks in town. An old credit union, a local chain, one Chase drive-through, and one giant old historic national trust.

That last one was just Stan's style.

He turned on the GPS and followed the prompts to Old Downtown – a four-block section of vintage city that seemed to be empty except for construction in nearly every building.

The street he ended up on dumped into the one that ran right down the front of the bank, the Belling National Trust. Art deco-style gray stone with twelve-foot-high windows covered in iron bars.

An alley ran down one side and connected to the one along the back that curved away in both directions. The line of shops across the street seemed empty. Apartments along the second floor.

As he passed the perpendicular street, he could see a statue a couple blocks down and one of those traffic circles around it. He cut down the first side street and bounced over rough brick until he found the alley he thought might be the one running behind the bank.

After turning down it and dodging the potholes, he found the rear of the bank. Blank stone on one side. A featureless white fence on the other. Two blue dumpsters choking off access to the street out front.

He continued on for several hundred yards before an intersection. An alley that took him out to the street he had started on that would take him back out front.

A parking garage on the corner caught his eye. Diagonal to the front door, it might offer a guy a good vantage point. Something with cover and several escape routes.

He filed it away for further consideration.

Past the shops again, and it looked like one of them might be open after all. A military surplus store on the end.

Haggis slid his truck into one of the angled spaces next to an old AMC Eagle. He got out and took a moment to admire the love and care that had gone into her. Somebody was proud of that little car for sure.

Creamy white with red pinstripes. Snowflake rims. A high stance. Tough and sporty at the same time.

He heard the jangle of a door opening behind him. Turned to find an older fella coming out of the surplus store with a cardboard box full of what looked like rubber gas masks. "She was one of the first passenger vehicles with four-wheel-drive."

Haggis nodded. "Yep. Almost unheard of back then. What ... '79?"

"That's right, and she was one of the first off the line."

"What's in her?"

"Just one option the first year. The 4.2-liter inline six. It was strange but cheap. Plenty of torque to get all the wheels spinning." He gently set the box down on the hood. Nodded at Haggis' truck. "Never been the biggest fan of GM, but the small block they put in their trucks was just about indestructible. Is that the 305 or the 350?"

Haggis chuckled. "I got the 400 in her. She runs about 250 horsepower, but it's the torque I wanted. A little over 400 foot pounds."

When the guy whistled in appreciation, Haggis stuck out his hand. "The name's Dan."

His grip was dry and strong. "Call me Pete."

Haggis pointed at the surplus store. "You shopping here?"

"Nope. I'm the owner."

"So you're open?"

Pete shook his head. "Unfortunately, no. Belling is doing some historic restoration of this whole stretch of buildings. Got the power shut down on this side of the street for six days, but I suspect it'll be longer. You leave something to the government and it gets screwy."

Haggis made his face sympathetic. "That's too bad. I'm in on business. Had some free time and was hoping to see something interesting."

Pete grinned. "You can look around all you want, but I can't take a credit card. Cash only, unless you got something to trade back there."

Haggis thought about his rifle. Not for sale at any price. He shook his head. "Cash is king where I'm from too."

Pete grinned and swept his arm at his storefront. "Then be my guest. Just let me stow this box, and I'll be along."

The hinges of the passenger door on the Eagle creaked and squealed. Maybe Pete just cared about the looks of the old girl and not her substance.

Haggis stepped inside to a familiar smell of oil and leather and aged dirt. Circular rows of uniforms and belts. Old metal from canteens to casings. Flags and bayonets.

A slapdash kind of logic, but it was so dark, Haggis

could barely see what was toward the back. Two cement pillars that held up the second floor made it even darker.

He turned around, and the front of the bank to the left of the entry door was centered in Pete's window. He stepped to the smaller window on the street side, and he looked up at the parking garage. He only saw two cars in it, but he could only make out their color. One red and one silver.

A black Dodge would have made him punch the wall.

Pete came through, and when Haggis turned around, he bowed. "Welcome to my humble store, sir."

Haggis laughed. "Thanks. You got some stuff all right."

Pete shrugged. "It's not so much. Just the trinkets and things the younger shoppers are looking for. The kind of kids that need something military to add to their wardrobe. It don't matter the significance, they just wanna look a certain way. Like when they think it's cool to wear that Che Guevera shit. A murderer as the face of counterculturalism."

"I guess things can come to mean different things to different people."

Pete looked like he had eaten a slice of lemon. "I suppose."

"Besides, the history of what he did is so far removed from today, it's possible they just don't know about him, except as the symbol of a movement."

Pete nodded. "And that's what all this is for. To satisfy those that don't know any better. You look like a man that knows better."

"I do."

"Military?"

"Marine Corps. A long time in, a long time ago."

"I understand."

Haggis spread his hands. "Thanks for letting me come in and look around, Pete."

"One like you that knows better wouldn't shop in a store like this anyway, but thanks for coming in, Dan."

Haggis stepped in for another shake, and when Pete took his hand, Haggis pointed at the Eagle over his shoulder. "Better adjust that hinge. She sounds like she's about to bind up."

Pete snorted laughter as he shook his head. "It's hard to keep up with her. Falling apart faster than her owner."

Haggis raised his eyebrows. "Cash *is* king."

"Oh no. I ain't selling her just 'cuz I haven't put some oil on a door hinge. I'll stick with her a little longer."

"Good man," Haggis said. "It was good meeting you."

When he got back in his truck, a plan was forming. He tried calling Stan, but it went to voicemail.

He pulled out into the empty street. Food, a six-pack, then back to the motel. He'd try again later.

Chapter Six

Gen's mind was in constant motion. Like a swirling wave rushing toward the shore, rolling back under itself, churning the sand into clouds that burst through the surface.

She sat up with a soft sigh. Careful not to disturb Mo as she got up, she grabbed his t-shirt and slid it on to be enveloped in his smell. The bottom hung down just past mid-thigh.

Mo snored behind her as she walked to the front door. Distances seemed off. Like she was going to hit it long before her eyes told her she was too close. She felt jet-lagged as she slipped the bolt. Snuck out into the cool night. Shut the door as softly as she could.

Her joints ached. Like she had been tensing her muscles for hours. Like trying to balance on a flagpole.

She just wasn't used to living this way. Not the running for her life part — though she definitely wasn't used to that.

It was the sudden change in her diet. A difference in

activity level. She had lost muscle. Gained a little fat. A lot of water. Her system was in revolt. Hormones all over the place.

It had started when they had first left Wildwood. But lately, the change had accelerated. She had been so lean for so long, she had rarely menstruated. For the first time in years, she had gotten her period two months in a row. A full-blown cycle. Like it had been before she had started training, back when she was still a teenager.

But this time … nothing. Except for being the same weeping emotional basket case.

She didn't realize she was crying until a breeze blew across her face.

There had been a lot of tension lately in everybody. Mo wasn't old yet, but she was younger than him. And her appetites were young. She released tension through sex, and he was accommodating.

But under these unusual circumstances, with the tension increasing daily, her need for release had increased, and even Mo had mentioned it.

Not in a critical way. Just as an observation.

Emotional stress. A lot of extra sex. Hormones coming back online after gaining a little body fat. No wonder she had missed a period.

Everyone was in danger, and now there was the possibility that the baby growing inside her was at risk too. More than the children they were trying to save from predators, now they had one of their own to worry about.

It made it even more important than ever that they stick to it. Do everything they can to see it through. But now Ronnie had decided to check out. Let the men do it so they wouldn't be distracted.

She gathered the shirt into her fists. It made her so

angry that an ally had suddenly changed her mind like that. A betrayal that burned through her chest.

But she still loved her. She leaned back on the wall next to the door, wished Ronnie could be here for her right now.

And like magic, Ronnie's door opened. She stepped out wearing a loose t-shirt, and Gen had to cover her smile. Stan wasn't as big as Mo. Ronnie had shorts on underneath.

When she looked over and saw Gen, her smile was tentative. "I couldn't sleep."

"Me neither."

Ronnie shrugged. "So much on my mind."

"I know."

Gen remembered being in college. Feeling down and wanting to talk to her mother. And like that, the phone would ring, and it would be her. Some kind of bond only women seemed to share.

Even though Ronnie changing her mind had felt like being abandoned, she was here now, right when Gen needed her. Without another word, she broke down. Terrible rending sobs as she held her arms out.

And Ronnie was there.

Everything that had been in her mind. All the frantic worry swirling around came out in a weeping babble of words. There was no way Ronnie was able to make heads or tails of what she was saying, but she listened.

That's what Gen needed. Somebody to listen. And when she had gotten enough control of herself to make sense, she would need understanding.

She knew Ronnie would have plenty of that too.

Gen dropped down to sit on the ground. Pulling the shirt tail down between her skin and the cold concrete.

Ronnie sat next to her with one arm around her shoulder, the other one stretched across to rub her thigh.

Gen realized she was still rambling. Put her hand on top of Ronnie's. Took a deep breath. "I'm sorry," she whispered."

"Why?"

Gen shrugged. "I don't know. I didn't want to put any more on you. There's enough to think about and worry about and do. You don't need me clouding it up even more."

"Come on," Ronnie said. "You're the best friend I ever had. The way you looked at me earlier made me think I might have lost you."

Gen gasped. Turned to take her face in her hands. The rough scars under her fingers reminded her how strong Ronnie really was. "No, no. Never."

Ronnie took Gen's hands from her face. "But I disappointed you so much."

"Yes, but you're also the best friend I ever had. I just didn't understand, that's all. And I still don't. But we'll work it out together."

"Exactly. Together."

Gen wiped her face. Leaned back to put her head on the wall. Her braid was loosening. It was about time for the ritual of letting it down and cleaning it. An all-day chore.

She sighed, slapping her hand down on the concrete next to her.

"What?" Ronnie said.

"I have to do something about my hair."

"That's what has you so emotional? Me disappointing you, and your hair?"

Gen saw Ronnie's smile and relaxed into laughter. One she had regained her composure, she felt like the crying had been an initial release that had gotten the worst of it out of her system, but the laughter had cleaned out the rest.

She felt refreshed, lightened.

Ronnie settled back. "I've thought about it some more. Watching you walk out in anger … and then when you were gone, Shawna told me I was wrong too – "

"She did?"

Ronnie giggled. "Yeah, she has a strong spirit. It's hidden under recovery and the kinds of habits victims develop, but she's strong. I can see why Ian is into her."

"Me too."

Ronnie pushed the fluff of her hair back. "So I thought about it."

"And?"

She shrugged. "I'll do whatever you do."

"Don't put this on me."

"No, that's not what I mean. I just think you're right. I think … it was selfish of me to think I could make him do what I wanted. He has his own convictions. He would have done the right thing after a … you know, just talking."

"I guess just because somebody is listing the options doesn't mean they'll take them."

"I know. But now it doesn't matter. I made him promise. And he doesn't hold it against me."

It was Gen's turn to hold Ronnie as she cried.

She finally sat up, wiped her face, and pushed her hair back again. "So then."

"What?"

Ronnie looked at her from the corner of her eye. "Now that you're in control, and I can actually understand what you're saying, what were you trying to tell me?"

"Oh." Gen thought back to when she had been crying into Ronnie's shoulder. Didn't feel like repeating it all, so she shrugged. "I'm pregnant."

Ronnie squealed and slapped both hands over her mouth. Her eyes were so wide, the leathery skin on her forehead was a series of thick lines. Scars crinkling over the bubble of flesh that was her nose. Her joy so evident, Gen wondered how she could have ever been angry at her.

Chapter Seven

Stan sat in the rickety dining chair as Shawna and Ronnie flitted around him with scissors and clippers and hair dye. That shit stung his nostrils and burned his eyes.

Mo and Gen were still in their room. He wasn't sure how they were going to disguise her. Half fairy princess, half linebacker. Maybe they could cut her Rapunztel braid. Unfortunately, every time somebody brought it up, she broke down.

They'd have to cross that long blonde bridge when they came to it.

Ian came through the front door. Shawna looked over her shoulder at him. Turned back around before he could see her looking, but Stan saw her smile. He had to duck his head to hide his own.

"This should do it," Ian said. He held out Stan's phone. It had a long wire hanging from the headphone jack. It went to a small plastic box that Ian set on the table.

He would be able to speak more freely now.

He dialed Haggis back. Got an answer almost immediately. "Hey, boss."

Stan did not like that "boss", but he kept his protest to himself. "Haggis."

"Yeah, so I been into town already. I assume your bank is that old historic one in Old Downtown?"

"You assume correctly."

"Yeah, a guy figured it was your style. Anyway, I got a couple ideas. Some information. I think we should meet, but I don't think I wanna tell you where we're staying right now."

"So Gustoff is with you?"

"She is."

"Is she okay?"

"She is."

Stan remembered her attitude when she was standing in front of his gun. No fear at all. "She's tough."

Haggis chuckled. "That she is."

Stan thought he might say something else, but the line remained quiet. Just the sound of the big man's breath. "So then where do you want to meet?"

"There's a coffee shop down the street from the bank. You know it? Place called Rush to Town?"

Stan sneered at the terrible name. "Clever, I guess, but no. I've only been to Belling once, and it was a while back, but I think I can find it."

"You good to be there in a couple hours?"

Stan looked at his watch. "Say, half past 11?"

"Roger that."

Stan hung up and handed the phone back to Ian. "He's got some info and some ideas."

Ian grinned. "That's awesome, 'cuz I got nothing."

Stan looked up at him from under his brow. "Is that true?"

"Not really."

"That's what I thought."

Shawna stepped back with a nod. "We had a productive brainstorming session last night."

"Is that right?" Stan said.

Ronnie slapped his shoulder. "Sit still."

He sighed. Submitted to their final touches, but before they were finished, Ian handed him the phone again. "It's dialing."

Stan nodded before holding the phone up to his ear. The connection clicked over to a pleasant female voice. "Belling National Trust, how may I direct your call?"

"May I speak with Mr. Clarke, please?"

"He's in a meeting. May I take a message?"

Stan smiled. "Could you tell him Frank Stanley is calling? I think he might want to take this one."

There was an indrawn breath followed by a heavy pause. "Just a moment, sir."

Stan shook his head.

"Sit still," Ronnie hissed.

The phone connected with a man's voice the next time. "Mr. Stanley?"

"Ah, Mr. Clarke. How are you?"

"I'm well, sir. Thank you for asking. How can I help you? This is unexpected."

"First off, this call is protected against electronic listening."

"Well, I appreciate that, sir … I don't think I can take advantage of that right now."

That meant there was somebody right there listening to his end of the conversation.

Stan wanted to shout at Shawna and Ronnie to leave him the fuck alone. Instead he closed his eyes. "I understand."

"Is there somebody there asking about me right now?"

"There is always interest in our services. We pride

41

ourselves on how we treat our customers. There are multiple inquiries nearly every day."

Somebody was definitely there now, and had been there for days.

Stan opened his eyes to find that Shawna and Ronnie were apparently done. He rolled his eyes in exaggerated relief. Then he focused on the phone. "What are the odds of me getting to my boxes?"

"I'm afraid that would be impossible, sir. You must be here in person to retrieve the contents of a safety deposit box. I am legally prohibited from handling the contents in your stead."

That meant they had somebody watching the vault too.

"Well, I guess I need to schedule an appointment."

"No need for that, sir. You are welcome here anytime."

There was a muffled sound. Then a distorted voice. Stan couldn't make out the words. As if somebody had their hand over the mouthpiece. Mr. Clarke was back with a deep sigh. "Perhaps it would be best if you did make an appointment."

Mr. Clarke must have been told to schedule something so they would know when to be there. Lazy. "Oh, it'll probably be in a couple of days. I'm not even in town yet."

"I see. Do you know when you are expected to arrive?"

Stan stifled laughter. "Let's see. Two days from now. About 6 in the morning. I'm staying at the Holiday Inn out on Route 23."

"That is a decent hotel, sir, but I can recommend something nicer."

"No, that won't be necessary. You have already exceeded my expectations."

"That is very kind, sir."

Maybe with Mr. Clarke feeding the office his bullshit

story about his arrival and lodging plans, they could have a few days of breathing room.

"I'll call when I make it in."

"Very good, sir."

He hung up, and Ian took the phone again. Disconnected the scrambler and slid them both in his pocket. "Let's just put 'em on ice for now."

Stan shrugged. "Fine by me. I got nobody to call anyway. Except maybe for a pizza."

Ian nodded on his way out. "I'll handle all outgoing calls if you don't mind."

Stan yelled at the closing door, "Just make sure it has extra cheese on it."

"No onions," Ronnie shouted.

Stan clapped his hands. "Well?"

Ronnie and Shawna looked at each other. Both of them with twitching mouths like they were trying to keep from laughing. Ronnie nodded and pointed to the mirror behind the TV. "You're done."

If the office had found out about Stan and his box, it wasn't because Mr. Clarke had been disloyal. He had made that clear on the phone. It was because they were listening. And they probably were putting pressure on him.

He was relieved as he stood. He had hoped Mr. Clarke was worth the money he had paid. It seemed like that was the case. Then his smile froze when he saw his reflection.

They had lightened his hair so it looked like it was turning gray. Thinned it out and raised his hairline a couple inches. Trimmed and shaped his beard into a thin mustache and a tiny triangular Imperial under his bottom lip.

"I look like Pancho Villa's perverted uncle."

"It's not that bad," Shawna said, trying not to smile.

"You have to admit," Ronnie said, "you look different."

"I look like I'm out on parole."

"Those gaudy Hawaiian shirts you wear will still work. They'll just give off a different vibe."

"Yeah, an 'I want to hang around playgrounds' kinda vibe."

The door opened, and Gen walked in. She burst into laughter when she saw him. He gasped in surprise.

She had not only cut her braid off, her hair was in a short bob. Even as the laughter doubled her over, Stan could tell she had been crying. He suspected she would be just as pretty with short hair as she was when it was long, but he also knew that wouldn't be a consolation.

He looked away to catch his reflection again. Shawna and Ronnie finally broke, and they were all in a little group hug, sharing the joke of his disguise.

When Mo came in, he didn't even flinch, seeming not to notice Stan's ridiculous appearance. His face was shell-shocked, and Stan didn't think it was about him, or Gen's hair. He dreaded what he was going to find out, but as soon as everybody calmed down, he would ask what was going on between him and Gen.

Or maybe he didn't want to know.

Chapter Eight

Jeanette held her case of notes under her right arm. Everything Mallory Black had given her. Plus everything she and Haggis had added.

Her left arm was entwined in his as he led her down the sidewalk to the coffee shop. She agreed Rush to Town was a bad pun, but she didn't hate the name as much as he did.

A pair of huge sunglasses and a baseball hat pulled low helped to hide the sickening bruise on the side of her face. She had laughed when she saw her reflection when they left the room. "They'll probably think you've been beating me."

"They will?" He looked so comically perplexed at the notion. It made the growing feeling for him grow to an overwhelming crescendo. It felt like love, but she was unwilling to admit to it just yet.

"You're a rather large man, and I'm a woman. Anybody will immediately think the worst."

"I wouldn't."

"But you're a good person."

"There are lots of good people out there."

"Yes, but they aren't walking arm-in-arm with a woman that looks like she just got the shit beat out of her for burning the tuna casserole."

"I don't even like tuna casserole."

She looked up at him in shock, unable to believe that he didn't see it, then she noticed his innocent smile. "You're fucking with me?"

"A guy's gotta admit to being a little perplexed, but once I figured out what you were saying, it made me too sad to think about. So, yes. I'm fucking with you."

She grinned as she leaned into him. "Keep doing it, then. It was fun."

They had slept in the same bed again last night. Still no sex. She was relieved but also a little frustrated. Even though she would have gone through with it, in spite of the pain in her face, it was good she was able to rest.

Another reason for her rising feelings. A man next to a woman still put together pretty good — if she did say so herself — and he had held off. And she got the feeling he would continue to wait for as long as it took for her to get comfortable with the idea.

Men like him were hard to find. Not only had she looked, but so had all the other women she had met and worked with. It seemed like a Disney fantasy to expect a man to at least be civil, let alone treat her with respect and dignity.

Maybe it was a trap. Maybe that's why he was alone. No other woman would fall for it.

Yet she held on all the way to the table, and even then she was reluctant to let him go.

She watched him wait for her to sit before dropping into his own chair. The aroma was divine.

"You want me to just get you a black coffee?" he asked.

"I can get my own."

"I know you can, but there's no need for both of us to stand up there."

"Then let me do it."

He leaned back and grinned. "Fine by me. Can a guy get something like a salted caramel latte? Extra cream?"

She looked down to hide her smile. "I think a girl can handle that."

"Well then, I'll wait right here."

She acted like she was offended. Drawing back and fluttering her hands under her face. "Why, you just want me to go so you can stare at my butt."

He shrugged. "It had crossed a guy's mind."

"Animal."

She stood and lifted her nose in the air. Twirled away like she was in a huff. When she turned around, he was staring. Pretended like he had been caught. Coughed and turned to look at the wall. Tapped his fingers like he was nervous.

It felt like something she would have done with someone she had been with for years. Somebody who was in tune with her rhythms. It was scary, thrilling.

When she got to the counter, she realized the barista had been speaking to her. She smiled in apology. "I'm so sorry. My mind was somewhere else."

"No worries," she said. There was a ring in her nose so big it dangled in front of her upper teeth. A tattoo of a wave of musical notes coming out of her collar. "I just asked if I could help you."

Jeanette saw the latte Haggis wanted on the menu and ordered two. She noticed the girl's gaze settle on the left side of her face. Good thing for the sunglasses, or the girl would have noticed her staring at the nose ring.

The lattes were served under a clear plastic dome.

Little wooden sticks for stirring already stuck down in. Thirteen fifty seemed a little much, but she hadn't taken a drink yet.

On her way back to her table, she passed a guy in a loud shirt. He looked like an old mechanic that hung out at local football games to watch the high school cheerleaders. After-shave so strong it made her stifle a sneeze on her forearm.

She slid into her seat, and Haggis reached over, but instead of taking his coffee, he took her hand. "I have to confess. After you turned back around, I kept staring at your butt."

She shook her head in mock disapproval. "You have a problem."

He took the offered cup. "In my defense, it's a nice one."

And now she was blushing. She tried to hide it behind the dome of whipped cream, but it was clear by his grin that he had already seen it.

"Hey," a voice said over her shoulder. She tensed as she looked behind her. The creep was coming toward their table, a steaming cup in his hand.

He wasn't looking at her though. He pointed at Haggis. "Do I know you?"

She turned to see Haggis' demeanor change to steel. "I don't know *what* you know, friend." His voice was the distant rumble of thunder.

"Yeah, you were a Marine, right?" He held up his hand in apology. "Wait. Once a Marine, *always* a Marine, right?"

Haggis nodded as he leaned forward to squint. "That's right. Do I know you?"

The stranger grinned. Shrugged as he took another step closer. "I don't know what you know, buddy, but I know this." He dropped down in the chair at the side of their table, and he pointed to his face. "If this fooled you, then I must say … I'm impressed."

Haggis grinned, looked around like he expected somebody to be watching. "I'll be damned."

Jeanette didn't understand. She stared at the guy. Then he looked at her straight-on. When she saw it, she could barely believe it.

She almost blurted his name out. Then she dropped her voice to a quick whisper. "Stan?"

Haggis laughed. "I guess I do know you."

Stan sat back like he was proud of his magic trick. Sipped his coffee. Then he sobered as he leaned toward her. "I'm so sorry that this led to you being hurt. We were all worried sick when we couldn't get through. I just … I hope you accept that. I am truly and deeply sorry."

She couldn't form any words. It wasn't his fault, but until this moment she hadn't realized that she'd been blaming him.

Haggis saved her by speaking first. "Well, for my part, I appreciate that. Not speaking for her of course, but a guy is still happy to hear it."

Stan nodded to Haggis, but then he looked back at her. It was clear he was going to sit there until she said something. "Thank you, Stan. I'll be honest. I thought you were an asshole because Mallory Black thought you were an asshole."

"And now?"

"I'm not sure, but Haggis says you're a good man. So I think I will think so too."

She was surprised to realize she meant it.

He closed his eyes and leaned back in relief. "Thank you. I promise it won't happen again."

"Damn right," Haggis growled.

She shook her head. "No, this is all too heavy. Too … dramatic. You're both like a couple of girls."

Stan raised one of his dyed eyebrows. "That's sexist, right?"

Haggis shrugged. "I don't know anymore. All I do is look at her butt."

Stan nodded. "I've taken a peek at it myself."

Haggis saluted in approval. "Nice."

Jeanette slapped the table. "That's quite enough of that. I take back what I said."

Haggis snapped his fingers. "A guy tried."

This was how she was going to be pulled out of her bad mood? Years of feeling sorry for herself and drinking too much. These two assholes?

They were so proud of themselves. Trading knowing smiles. She couldn't help but laugh.

When she finally stopped, Stan leaned on his elbows like he was exhausted. "If you're finished, can we get to business?"

"Please," she said.

She was surprised to find that she liked him. A little disappointed too.

Chapter Nine

Ian sat at the small desk by the door. One of the few places in the room that didn't seem covered in cigarette smoke residue.

His workstation was open in front of him. Two tablets next to it. One digital, one old-fashioned lined paper.

Shawna and Mohammed had their work spread out on the dinette table. All the evidence from Jeanette Gustoff. Everything Household Services had uncovered. Assembled into a narrative. Timelines. Additional images for reference. Like they were doing a last-minute paper for a picky professor.

He was less concerned about their project and more involved in his own. A personal goal that he knew would quickly become an obsession if he let it.

Tracing the digital signatures of the other Household Services contractor. Cross-referencing the times with captured audio bursts similar to what he would expect from a scrambled signal.

And like one of those 3D puzzles that come to life

when you stare at them just right, he saw it, the pattern he was looking for.

He pumped his fist and whooped at the ceiling. "I got 'em."

He looked over, and Mohammed looked back like he was waking up from a nap. Shawna smiled at him. "Of course you did."

Her confidence in him was like a foregone conclusion. He wanted to go stand her up and kiss her until she ran out of breath, but he retired her smile and then jumped up to close his laptop.

He powered down his equipment and grabbed his ball cap off the chair. "I'm taking the van out. I'll check in every fifteen."

He didn't look back on his way out. He was afraid she would still be watching him.

One of these days … maybe after this job — after they re-established their dominance over the other contractors — he would tell her.

He wore jeans, a plain work shirt, and brown hiking boots. After the cold rain in Florida a week ago, the dry heat making the morning air heavy felt like a blessing. He worked better when it was hot.

He set up his equipment on the center console. This one was an older van, and the engine access was under the shroud between the two front seats. He always heard it called a doghouse.

Now that he knew what he was looking for, the signal bursts were easy to find and track. Of course it was coming from Old Downtown. He shook his head in disgust. The other contractor was probably parked right in front of the bank.

When he found out he was almost dead right, he couldn't feel good about it. He had assumed the competition would be low-rent hacks. It made things easier, just not challenging.

His equipment led him right to a white van parked a block down from the bank on the other side of the street, in front of a giant structure of scaffolding rising along the face of a building under construction. He couldn't tell if it was new or renovations. He cut into a parking lot marked for construction vehicles only. Trucks and vans and SUVs. All the way to the back next to the large air handlers cut into the block wall of the building next door.

In the rearview mirror he could see activity in the interior of the building behind him. Workers carrying materials and supplies, the sparks from cutting metal. Perfect.

He crawled into the rear of the van and dug in the box of props for a hardhat and an orange vest. He thought about the clipboard, grabbed the roll of paper instead. A set of blueprints for the Death Star on the inside. Innocent white paper held by several rubber bands on the outside.

Slid his equipment into a small backpack.

He hopped out and walked across the lot. Everything in his van was shut down. He was hidden from the other van's view. Unless they jumped out and blew their cover, it was unlikely he would be seen by anybody but the crew inside the building. And even then, so many people came and went on one of these jobs, it was unlikely he'd get stopped.

Just walk with your head up like you're looking for something. Nod every once in a while. Move like you know where you're going. If you catch somebody looking at you — a small smile and a nod of greeting — then back to business.

He found a set of stairs. All metal inside a stairwell of poured concrete. No door yet. Wires hanging out of conduits ready for lights to be installed. The higher he went , the less activity he encountered.

On the fifth floor – well above scenic Old Downtown – he saw a worker threading pipe in a corner. Gave him a small salute before moving to the front of the building. Looked down on the street, just past the scaffolding, to see the roof of the van.

He slid his backpack off. Dropped to his knees in front of the window and pulled the equipment out. Measured the signal coming from the van and confirmed it was the signal he was looking for.

Somebody was in it right now. Listening. Searching. Sniffing out information.

They must have paid somebody for the spot out front to have easy access to the bank. An easy escape if they get discovered.

He could record what was coming from the van. Hide his own communications in the gaps of their security. He'd be like a mouse crawling along the baseboard. Just the occasional scratching noise. Gone too fast to be seen.

He pulled his phone out for a couple of pictures. The van in context, in reference to the position of landmarks. The fire hydrant, the manhole cover. He'd come by and check it tomorrow to see if it moved, or if they were leaving it in its spot overnight. That would tell him if he needed to look for another vehicle they were using.

After capturing enough data for an accurate digital fingerprint, he shut down. Slapped his laptop closed a little harder than was probably good for it. As he packed back up, his smile faltered when he heard the scrape of boots on the bare floor.

"How's it going?" a voice said. Not confrontational, but he still had to be careful.

He looked up to find a man standing over him.

Nothing to say where he was in the organizational structure of the construction company. Foreman? Drone? Ian grinned. "Pretty good. How about yourself?"

"Oh, I'm all right. You from the county? We was supposed to get that gas inspector in."

Ian shook his head. "Sorry, no. I'm from Belling Com. City Council's wanting to set up a free Wi-Fi zone to cover Old Downtown. Just surveying line-of-sight options."

The guy straightened in confusion. "Wouldn't that be better from the roof?"

Yes. It would have been.

Ian pulled his head in and spread his hands. "It's the tallest building for several blocks." He sighed. "I'll be honest —"

The guy held up his hand. Shook his head as he smiled. "I gotcha. You just didn't want to haul your crap up the ladder."

Ian took a relieved breath. "Exactly. It's a self-contained transceiver. Solar-powered. Just plop it down and run some bolts through it." He hooked his thumb over his shoulder to point out into the street. "The most important thing is making sure there's a signal to the bank."

He looked where Ian was pointing and rolled his eyes. "That thing has caused more trouble than you could believe. We had to shut down this whole side of the street for a week. Instead of both at once for a single day."

"No kidding?"

"We can only shut power down on the other side at night. You have any idea what that costs in overtime?"

So he was in management. Ian whistled in appreciation. "I've had to reschedule my team to get inside for a utility audit four times. I was wondering why I couldn't pin them down."

He stood and slung his backpack back on. "I bet if it

was them asking, your county man would have been on time."

The guy laughed. "We're all out of Austin. Bidding on jobs there is a headache, let me tell you, but this small-town shit is giving me cramps."

Ian started toward the stairs. "Try living here."

The guy followed. "No thank you."

At the top of the stairs, Ian turned to walk through the door backward. "How about when I get to the office, I'll see if I can find out about our gas inspector."

His face brightened. "Hey, thanks."

Before he could realize Ian hadn't asked for any contact information, he waved. Spun around to skip down the stairs. He almost laughed in relief when he looked up at the bottom of the first flight to see he wasn't coming down after him. At least not at the same speed.

Still nobody followed when he got outside. He jumped into the van. Kept his hardhat on as he pulled into the street, craning his neck to see past the other van. Dark windows making the rear look like a skull.

Chapter Ten

Mo felt ridiculous in his disguise. A wig of long frosted dreadlocks under a knit beanie. Sunglasses and sandals to finish an outfit of dirty tank top and cargo shorts.

The hair itched and stank.

When he had been a Breacher in the Army, he had become familiar with how to blow up barriers. Doors, concrete pillars, walls. He shuffled down the sidewalk in front of the abandoned shops across from the bank, looking into the windows, trying to look too much like a hobo.

At the Belling Military Surplus window, he looked in to confirm what Haggis had told him. Completely open except for a couple of large concrete columns.

A little bit of Det-Cord and some C4, and they could come down like an avalanche. A bunch of damage and a spectacular display, but nobody gets hurt. Just fireworks to freak the locals out. To confuse anybody else that might be watching.

He walked back down the sidewalk. Past the shops and to the big building being built or torn down, he couldn't tell. Plastic flapping from the scaffolding. A white van right in front of it, more vans just like it in the parking lot.

The coffee shop was directly across from it.

Nothing good here. It might go either way if he tried to drop it. Or injure some soccer mom coming in for a pumpkin-flavored doughnut. It looked like his best bet was going to be the surplus store on the corner. The other shops like a padding in that direction. A street with a parking garage in the other. Nothing but parking behind it. The bank set back off the sidewalk across the street.

Those tasty columns inside. Shelves and glass and old ceiling tiles. Blow all that out into the street in a gap in traffic. Whatever traffic there might be. He'd been piddling around for a half an hour and could count the cars that had passed on one hand.

Back to the surplus store for a final look, but another window caught his attention. A display of baby clothes. He looked past his reflection to stare at the tiny socks.

Maybe Gen wasn't really pregnant. It's not like she took a test. She just said she knew she was pregnant. Could feel it.

But he had to believe it. Or at least to act like it was true. It changed the way he had to plan for everything. Not just the job of getting the evidence for the bank, but for after.

If there was an after.

He broke away from the baby clothes. It wouldn't do for somebody to call the cops on a large black man looking into the window of a store that sold second-hand onesies.

He went back to the corner. One last look inside the surplus building. He wouldn't have to worry about alarms. With the power shut off, entry would be easy. The owner was probably counting on the fact that it wasn't common knowledge, though he'd told Haggis readily enough.

Mo stepped off the curb to cross the street to the parking garage. Almost tripped when his foot came down on the toe of the sandal. Froze in mid-stride to fix it before it could send him tumbling to his face. Stayed rooted to the asphalt when he looked up and saw a black Dodge sitting in the alley between the parking garage and the building next to it. A stubby brown block with two roll-up doors on the front, a corner made of windows. Belling Transmission.

He looked away. Dropped down to adjust the sandal. Glanced up as he tightened the strap. He wanted to see if it was one from the office, or if it was just a black Charger.

Parked like it was on a stakeout?

He held his wig on as he slipped the beanie off. Stood up and started back across the street, weaving like he was unsteady. Drugs or booze. An easy picture to paint.

When he cut toward the car, he squinted at the windshield. Making it look like he was trying to see inside. Thick tendrils of matted hair hung in front of his face.

He only saw one person inside. Was there another nearby? Taking a dump in the weeds? Did it matter?

Mo decided that it did not. He remembered how Ronnie had trembled in his arms after rescuing her in her apartment. What these men were going to do to her. What they wouldn't hesitate to do to Gen, or her baby.

He picked up his pace a few steps from the car and reached out with his beanie.

The window hummed down. "Keep stepping, dreads." The voice was rough and pitched low for menace. Mo wanted to laugh.

"Lemme get this, boss." He started buffing little circles in the windshield.

A hand came out the window, palm to the sky. "Fuck off!"

Mo staggered to the side past the open window like he was going to fall down. Caught himself on the post to look in the car, dreadlocks spilling inside. "Come on, boss. I'm tryna eat."

The door swung open, pushing Mo back. He threw his arms out like he was losing his balance. "Eat this," the guy shouted, and as he got out, he reached under his jacket.

Trying to be a big man with a big gun. Scaring off somebody he saw as a victim.

Mo pushed off the wall behind him. Planted his sandal in the center of the guy's chest. His mouth was a perfect circle. Eyes in slits. Eyebrows climbing into his hair.

He folded back into the car, the back of his head thumping off the top edge of the door frame. Mo followed him in to grab a lapel in each hand. Dragged him forward to drive his knees into his solar plexus. Stepped back and put both hands on the top of the guy's head. Held it there to bring his knee up into his chin.

He caught him before he crumpled to the ground. Spun him around. Slapped his hands down as he tried to fend him off.

Mo slammed his head in the door. Once was all he needed. He leaned in to look for the trunk release. Popped it open. Squatted down to retrieve the weapon the guy had been reaching for. Tossed it on the seat. Went through the pockets. Found nothing just like he suspected he would.

Dragged the guy to the back. Threw him in like a bag of mulch. Grabbed the yellow internal release handle with both hands. Gave it a good yank that lifted the rear-end off its shocks, tearing the handle off at the base.

Tossed it in and closed the trunk.

When he slid into the driver's seat, he pulled the dreadlock wig off with a moan of pleasure. Scratched his head for several seconds before closing the door.

The guy had been sitting in a closed car without the AC. In a sports coat.

Mo shook his head as he pulled out. Kicked on the air before rolling the window up. He was supposed to meet Haggis in the parking lot of the Belling Family Drug. Just a couple of blocks down. He could still do it, he would just have a friend with him.

He looked in the rearview mirror, but only saw his own eyes. They tightened as he shook his head. Looked out both sides. Didn't see anybody following, but he realized it may not matter. He was certain the guy hadn't been able to call anybody, but he was a fool if he thought they wouldn't notice one of their operatives was missing.

He pulled into the small lot behind the drugstore. Pulled to the end farthest from the street. When he shut it down, he kept the windows up. Suddenly it didn't seem so weird.

Chapter Eleven

Haggis had spent a full day looking for his spot, a place with a high vantage point. Hidden, with an easy retreat. He had ruled out the building under construction almost immediately. Even with the power out and Old Downtown about to close for some historic update, it was crawling with workers.

The parking garage was mostly empty. Only a few cars. The occasional pedestrian cutting through the bottom level. He had just needed to find a spot inside it.

He had walked all day. When he found out the garage was mostly used for overflow parking from the ball field six blocks away, he knew it was his place.

Every level from front to back, looking for signs of urban campsites, teenage gatherings. It seemed to be low on the list of party locations, so he focused on the side facing the street that ran by the bank. Edging closer toward the front corner.

The roof level was too high and had no cover. The one right below it — the third floor — was better, but a tree obscured most of his view. Not ideal, but it might afford him something to hide behind if there was nothing else.

At least the branches spread apart and allowed him to see through it. The second and first floors had zero view through the tree. Even if he found a place that hid him while trying to provide cover for Stan as he went into the bank, it was no good if he couldn't see.

Walking along the outside edge near the railing, he found a small niche between a concrete utility room and a support pillar, only accessible from where he had been walking. No cigarette butts or empty cans, just a few dry leaves and dirt in the corners. Like it was undiscovered.

He had to turn sideways to get into it. When it widened slightly inside, he could turn around. He thought it might work.

He dropped a twenty dollar bill on the ground at the base of the rear wall. If he came back and it was still there, it meant nobody had used the space. It didn't guarantee that nobody ever did, but it was a small assurance that he would remain hidden.

His luck would have somebody show up right when he was getting set up to fire.

On his way back out, he could see through the tree to the front of the bank. A full view of the entry doors all the way to the corner where the alley started.

He went back to the motel where Jeanette waited for him. They went out like young lovers, hand-in-hand and leaning on each other's shoulders. Back to the room for some drinks and conversation, and they fell asleep side-by-side like they had been doing it for years.

Still no sex, and as difficult as it was becoming, there was something fun and mysterious about it.

Like they were learning to live with each other without it first. Probably something more couples should do.

Necking like kids parked on Lookout Hill. Pulling apart with twin gasps of pleasure and disappointment.

The next morning, he dropped Mo off a few blocks down and drove to park at a Provisions off the town square. Walked all the way to his spot in the parking garage. Pressed back into the alcove to find his twenty sitting undisturbed. Turned to look through the gap in the trees to confirm the view. He could rest the barrel of his rifle on the railing just past the edges of his hiding spot. With his suppressor, nobody would see the muzzle flash, and only somebody right outside the structure would be able to pinpoint the source of the shots.

With Mo's distraction causing a ruckus, he should be able to get out undetected.

He made a circle with his hands to look through. Scanned to the limits of his narrow view. Slowed his breathing and imagined sighting in on an enemy.

A black blob moved into his circle. He drew back to see it was a Dodge Charger, driving toward the left. Nothing but the rear entrance to the garage, and an alley.

He waited to see if they were patrolling, driving up one level at a time. When he heard nothing he emerged from hiding and walked to the railing on the side that faced the military surplus store. Looked for the car before carefully leaning out and checking both directions. He saw the nose of the Charger poking out from the alley to the right. He couldn't tell if it was running.

Before pulling back, he saw Mo step out from under the awning of the surplus store. His heart beat in his throat. He couldn't tell if Mo saw the car or not. When it looked like he tripped stepping into the seat, Haggis whirled away.

He could run the long way around the ramp, or the

slightly shorter way of making it all the way to the rear corner and coming down the stairs.

By the time he got to the stairwell, he was already out of breath. It seemed like a bad idea, but it was too late to take the other route. He stumbled down the first flight. Grabbed the rail to keep on his feet. When he made it to the bottom, his hands were cramping and his ankles were on fire.

He forced himself into a lumbering sprint. Slowed at the corner near where the Dodge was parked. Hit the wall and leaned out to get one eye past the edge. He jerked back when the car pulled into the street.

He waited until the sound of the engine faded. Then he looked out to see it shrinking in the distance, then turning left down a side street.

He threw himself over the railing. Almost hooked his toes on the top, but he made it. Landed on his feet with his hands down for balance. He rushed to get his feet up to speed before falling on his teeth, but when he got to the alley, nobody was there.

He spun in a circle. Then bent over his knees to catch his breath when dizziness hit.

Did they have him? Was Mo dead in the trunk? Or had it been just a regular old Dodge Charger, and Mo had walked by to the other end of the alley?

Haggis stood up straight, fighting the stitch forming in his side. Headed in the same direction the car went. He would soon get to the Provisions, to his truck and see if Mo made it to the drugstore. Then ... he wasn't sure what he would do if Mo didn't show up.

A measured drive the few blocks to where he was supposed to meet him, and in the parking lot was the Charger. He had already pulled in, and the lot wasn't quite big enough to just turn around. He'd have to finesse it out of there. Pulled to the end, keeping his face turned away from the Dodge but his gaze on it from the corner of his eye. As he backed into a slot, the driver's door opened.

When Mo popped out and jogged over, Haggis realized his truck was still moving, even though he had frozen in confusion. Slammed on the brakes before he hit a light post and waited for Mo to jump in.

He pulled away without putting his foot through the firewall and made it out of the lot without hitting anything. He waited for Mo to say something but finally had to break the silence. "Did you steal that car?"

"Kind of, yeah."

"Was anybody in it when you did?"

"Yeah, but he was in the trunk."

"How? I mean …"

"Well, I fractured his skull with the door after he tried to shoot me."

"He tried to shoot you?"

"Well, he threatened to. Look, he was gonna shoot me for sure. Or try eventually."

"Oh." Haggis loosened his fingers. Looked around like he was just becoming aware he was behind the wheel. "So, should we leave it there?"

"Why not? It might be a day or two before somebody discovers it with the way parking is around here. Cars just *everywhere*."

"It's the construction."

"Yeah, but that ain't what worries me."

"What?"

"If he was supposed to check in, it ain't gonna happen. I may have fucked up and tipped our hand."

"No, he's already hurt somebody. Part of the requirements of working for these motherfuckers. A guy can get behind a little house cleaning. I say we take it as it comes."

Mo clapped his hands. "My man."

Haggis was ready to get this all over with. The sooner they could make it happen, the sooner he could put all his attention on Jeanette.

Chapter Twelve

Ronnie only had herself to blame. She hated having nothing to do. Had been complaining about it for weeks. Stared arguments forced Stan to put her into his plans … and though she had talents and abilities, what could she do really?

She helped with his disguise. Supported him and listened to him when he needed to unload. All the things she guessed a good wife was supposed to do. She just wasn't a wife.

She never knew how boring being on the run could be. Hopping between her room and Gen's. Both identical, and ratty. She was ashamed to admit that she had gotten used to better, and she missed it.

The same conversations. The same worry. To the point that the anxiety calmed by virtue of her inability to pay attention to it, like staring at an abstract painting.

People coming and going. All familiar and nice. All boring.

Being on the edge of panic for so long was exhausting. She needed a release.

Every time Stan came in she jumped him and tried to drag him to bed. Sometimes he relented, but mostly … he was too busy.

And Texas was different from Florida. So dry it felt like it was sucking the water right out of her. Her skin felt like an old alligator bag. She'd been putting so much moisturizer on her face, it was like she had been bathing in lard.

Everybody had an essential skill, something that made them indispensable. She felt like all she had was her body, and she was only willing to use it for one of them.

Just as she scolded herself for being so dramatic, the door opened. Even though Stan looked like an aging hipster, she threw herself into his arms with a squeal. He laughed into her mouth as they kissed.

He put her on her feet and pulled her to the door. She resisted, trying to steer him in where she could have him to herself, but he was too strong.

She relented, and he took her outside. A slow walk along the front of the motel. "Where are we going?" she asked.

"Around," he said. Pulled her closer to drop his arm over her shoulder.

They walked past the front office. She had been in there once, and the AC was cranked so high she thought she might be able to see her breath.

Stan led her to a small picnic area off the side of the parking lot. To a patio table under a faded umbrella. A cooler sat on the table. A bottle of white wine sitting down in the ice, two glasses resting in the shade.

She let him lead her to a seat. "What is this?"

He waited for her to sit before dropping down across from her. "It's a special day."

"Is it?"

He nodded as he opened the wine. Pour them each a glass.

"Why is it important?"

He tapped the rim of his glass against hers. "Because it might be the last."

The mysterious joy building inside her bled out with her sigh. "Well, isn't that just the most positive thing I've ever heard."

He grinned. His mood was at odds with his words. "We're so close to seeing this thing done. And I have to give you a toast. If not for you ... I can't honestly say I would have gone through with it. But I can honestly say that I'm better because of you. That if we succeed, any girls we save are because of you."

She looked down at the charred grass. "That's not true."

"But it is. Every positive step I've taken, every change I've made, all the good things in my life right now are because of you. So there's that."

She felt like people were watching her. "I don't know if that's true."

He shrugged. "You don't have to know it. It's what I believe, and what I'll tell anybody that will listen."

"Why?"

"Because I love you."

He had said it often enough, but this time it felt different. It had a strength, a heaviness. Was it his voice or her mood that made it sound that way?

"I love you too." She took a drink, swallowing more than a mouthful and holding her hand under her chin in case she couldn't get it down. Caught her breath through a coughing fit and laughed in embarrassment.

Stan waited patiently for her to recover, taking

measured sips as an example. His small smile looking like he knew a secret he was about to reveal to the world.

Ronnie set her glass down and wiped her hand on her shorts. "Is this what you've really been doing? Instead of planning this out, you've been stashing wine for this ... depressing conversation?"

He pretended to take offense, covering his heart with both hands. "Confessing my love is depressing?"

"No, the other stuff about it being the last day."

He sobered before picking his glass back up. "We have to be a hundred percent honest with each other, babe. I'm going into that bank tomorrow, and I may not come out. Somebody might find us. Kill us in our sleep. We may finish the job and then have an unfortunate accident. They killed a senator — almost on live TV. If they got their shit together, would they hesitate to drop a plane out of the sky if they thought we were on it?"

She knew she didn't need to answer that question. She poured more wine. "But there is a chance that everything will work out, right?"

"Yes. That's why we are going to finish this wine, and then I'm going to show you something."

When they had first gotten together years ago, she would have been uncomfortable just looking into his eyes. She felt like she could do it all day now. When the bottle was empty, she could have sat with her hands in his, staring until the sun went down, but he pulled her to her feet.

She thought he was going to lead her back to the room. Finally take her up on the offers she had been making most of the day, but at the front office he stopped, opened the door, and waited for her to step inside.

The air chilled the sweat on her exposed skin, and she suppressed a shiver. There was a common area to the right.

A few greasy tables, a snack machine, and a community TV.

The tables had been pushed to one side. Chairs stacked neatly. Birthday candles sitting on squares of tape. Burning in competition with the sun coming in the front windows. Soft music coming from a Bluetooth speaker. "Is that Frank Sinatra?"

He led her to the middle of the impromptu dance floor. "Harry Connick, Jr."

Brought her close until she was against his chest. Tipped his head to lay his cheek on the top of her head. Guided her back and forth in the only dancing he knew how to do. "I want to make you a promise," he said.

She was afraid to talk. She could only nod, wondering if she was making his shirt look oily.

"I want to learn to dance, with you, whenever you want, whatever type of dancing you want. No more of this Fonzie shit. Just swaying when the music is slow enough. I don't want to do that anymore. Or not just that. I want more. I want it all."

She closed her eyes. "Okay."

"If tomorrow is not the day I hope it to be, I want you to know these are my intentions, to be with you forever. But I need to know you will be here. I need to be certain that I can wake up a year from now and feel your hair tickling my face."

She pushed away from him and wiped her tears as she looked up. "What are you saying?"

He stomped his Everyday Carry. "I'm not going to get on my knee. Forgive me for that, but I guess this isn't the most conventional proposal as it is."

"You're asking me to marry you?"

"I am. Just one more thing to look forward to. Something else to fight for. I'm ready for this. I want this. So yes. Will you marry me?"

She stepped back and opened her arms. "When did you do all this?"

"I didn't. Gen and Shawna did it. A little short notice, and Ian grumbled a bit until he saw how excited Shawna was, and then he was all for it."

Ronnie shook her head. "He's hopelessly in love with that girl."

Stan grabbed her hands and pulled her back into the slow dance. "And I'm hopelessly in love with *this* one."

Another song came and went, and they still hold each other. He reached behind her to scratch her back, and she had to stop moving so she could moan in pleasure. "You haven't answered me?"

"Do I need to?" she said.

"I think so. I mean, you made me ask."

"Yeah, I guess so."

"Then what do you say?"

She stretched under his hands. "I just did."

"Oh, you guess so?"

"Yes."

"Then I guess I'll take it."

Shuffling footsteps behind her brought them both to a stop. They separated and turned to see the owner of the motel standing in the doorway. Dom Hayes. Short, obese, unwilling to admit he was going bald.

She hadn't actually met him, but she had been told he was … unpleasant.

"You gonna clean this shit up soon?"

Stan burst out laughing. Bent to give Ronnie a kiss before answering. "We were just finished."

Ronnie put her hands on her hips. "Bullshit. We were just getting started."

She pulled Stan back into their dance. Like he had said, this might be their last day.

Chapter Thirteen

As much as Stan loved bad food, he was past the need for it. Being on the run was bad for his health. Not just from the threat of a bullet, but creeping hypertension. An extra few pounds slowing him down.

Open pizza boxes piled on top of each other. He had eaten more than his fair share. Ronnie and Gen had taken one next door. Gen glaring at him over her shoulder as she left. A look that told him he better not leave her out of the final stage of planning.

He knew Gen would eat far more than Ronnie. Even without the obsessive exercise, she was still a big machine.

Ian was the big surprise of the night. Putting it away on pace with Mo.

Shawna and Mohammed were back at their temporary headquarters in the motel across the street. Stan wondered how much they had eaten. Shook his head at himself. What a dumb thing to have take up space in his mind.

He leaned back and looked between Ian and Mo to see the rundown room behind them. Though he had been in worse places, he couldn't help feeling like he needed a shower. It felt more like they were planning on robbing a drug dealer. Small-time crooks trying to knock over a tiny farm bank in a Midwest shithole.

He closed his eyes and massaged the bridge of his nose. "The hardest part is still going to be walking away." He opened his eyes to find Ian smiling.

"We just have to make sure the path is clear." Ian pointed at Mo. His explosion cuts off approach from that corner. Nobody can get through to that end of the street, coming or going. That leaves the street coming from the town square. I think I can turn 'em away by dumping the other contractor's van into traffic."

Mo leaned forward and put his finger on the table. "How does disabling the van block traffic? You gonna drive it across the lanes?"

"Nope. You're going to build me a charge that will tip it over into the street."

Mo's grin was wide and eager. "That's news to me, but I accept."

Stan took a drink of his Corona. Had to stop himself from thinking about Frank. They had often sat on the beach with a cooler full. Maybe he should switch brands. "So nobody can get to the front of the bank, but they can still get into the alley on the near side. Or come from the other direction."

Mo nodded. "Haggis said there were some big dumpsters in the alley. As soon as I park back there, push 'em across the alley. That isolates the bank from every direction. If you get done quick enough, we can be out the back before anybody comes for us."

Ian laughed. "Who? Everybody is busy with the panic from the explosions?"

"Everybody who? That place is deserted because of the

construction. Power's out on that whole other side of the street."

"Gen and I will figure that out," Stan said.

Mo turned to meet Stan's gaze. "Excuse me?"

"She'll be driving."

"Fuck no."

Stan shrugged his hands. "*You* can't do it."

"That's what we planned."

"How?" Ian asked. "You'll be across the street setting the surplus store off. Haggis will be up in his watchtower covering you while you make it to the car that's already in the alley."

"I'll get there early."

Stan sighed. "You and Haggis will be at the parking garage in the Honda. You'll be there early. Across the street. Gen will bring me in the Subaru."

Mo gritted his teeth as he sat back. "And what about Ronnie?"

"She'll be here."

"Oh, your woman gets to be safe?"

Stan slammed his fist down on the table. "Do you really fucking think any of us are safe after tomorrow?"

Mo looked away, shaking his head.

"Besides," Stan said. "Jeanette is staying in their room. Shawna and Mohammed are staying behind."

"Why aren't they coming?"

Ian reached for another piece of pizza. "They got the server ready to broadcast. They keep it live so when we come back with the video, they can slipstream it into the multimedia packet they designed — it's really nice, by the way. Like a segment on Oprah."

"That's right," Stan said. "And we'll likely have bad guys chasing us or already on their way here. The last knock on the door Ronnie hears might be the one right before she gets shot in the head."

Mo held his hand up. "Okay, I get it. But she ain't driving back. Once I get over there, I get behind the wheel."

"Fair enough."

Stan nodded. "So, it comes down to me getting in and out without trouble. Or with a minimum …" He paused to sigh. "Hell, even a *moderate* amount of trouble, as long as I get out alive."

The following silence was broken only by Ian's loud chewing.

Stan lifted his bottle for another drink only to see it was empty. He set it back down with a sigh. "My instincts are to keep them out of danger. To protect them at all costs. But let's say I get shot coming out of the bank. Let's say *you* get shot coming across the street. Let's say we both die."

Mo rotated to throw his arm over the back of his chair. "Okay. We both die." He looked at the front door. "We wouldn't be around to protect them anyway."

Ian laughed. "Assuming you need to."

Stan imagined Gen and Ronnie on the run together. They'd probably get farther than he gave them credit for. "You're right. In which case they didn't *need* protection anyway."

Ian tossed his uneaten crust back into the box. "Bingo."

"Okay," Mo said. "Okay. She drives you to the bank. Haggis is leaving his truck here, but I ain't going in it. I'll ride with him in the SUV. I'm coming to you, and we all come back *together*."

Ian smiled as he cleaned grease from his nails on a napkin that looked like it was out of dry spots. "Well, I got a local guy — an independent contractor. He will be sending a courier to drop off some supplies in an hour or so." He turned to Mo. "I think you will be excited to see it. It's all your favorite stuff."

"How do you know what my favorite stuff is?"

"I don't. I just remember how excited you were when you asked for it." He looked at his watch. "So, if you gentlemen will excuse me."

He walked out like there was nobody else in the room.

Mo turned back to the table after the door closed. "He acts like he's the star quarterback."

Stan wiped his face with one of the remaining napkins. "It does feel like a fraternity around here. Pizza, beer, and marginally clean sheets. Did Gen tell you about me and Ronnie?"

Mo nodded. "She did. Congratulations."

Stan shrugged. "Thanks, but I don't know if it was the right thing to do."

"Why?"

"I don't know. I just don't want her to think I did it just because … "

"Because you think we're gonna die, and it won't matter? Like it was an empty gesture?"

"That's right."

Mo pushed off the table to stand. "You are fucked up, man. The worst thing to happen is we make it out of this alive, and you end up living the rest of your life with somebody you love. What an empty gesture."

He followed Ian out, leaving Stan to clean up the aftermath of their lunch.

He wasn't afraid of dying, of Ronnie having to go on without him. He was afraid she would die, and he would have to go on without her.

Even if they got out of this, somebody would be coming for them. They would always be looking over their shoulder. Would it be enough for her that they were looking together?

Chapter Fourteen

Gen took the little Subaru Ian had gotten for them to the bank. It was quicker than it looked, had more room in it than expected.

She was tickled to be driving the car, at least to the bank if not back to the motel. And she was fine with that. She had something to do — even as small a part as it was — and it was about time. She had asked enough times. Even had a near argument with Ronnie about it.

It still made sense to go to and from a couple of times just in case. God forbid if something happened to Mo, and she had to drive back. But with or without him, she would do it.

That's why she had agreed with Ronnie. It didn't matter if they all died as long as those girls were saved. At least one of them. What was this all for otherwise?

There had been an argument of course. Mo didn't want to let her do it.

"Let me," she had yelled. "I don't need your permission, Moses White. I don't even need you to understand."

"So what I say doesn't matter?"

"Not right now, no."

He put his hands on his hips. Nodded his head like this is what he had been waiting for. "So this is how it's going to be."

"What does that mean?"

"Just you doing whatever you want, and I'm supposed to just let you walk all over me?"

It was so ludicrous, she couldn't stop herself from laughing. So hard she snorted like a pig. She often did it when a joke took her by surprise.

His mouth twitched like he wanted to smile too, but his eyes were too confused. It only made her laugh harder. "How did you get there?" she asked.

"What do you mean?"

"Me wanting to have a part in this thing — wanting to do my part — to me walking all over you? You're mad because you think I've taken something away from you? Like your manly dignity? Like I should just sit behind and do what I'm told and never question you because as the man, you know best?"

He threw his hands out. "Well no. That just sounds ridiculous."

She covered her mouth with both hands, and she could see him struggling to keep his face straight. He finally broke, and they both laughed.

He took her into his arms. "Yes. That's exactly what I was thinking. But it was so I could be the one to get in front of it. So you would be protected behind me."

"Am I really safe though?"

"I don't know. I can only do my best and pray. But if you were behind, then at least I wouldn't have to worry about you as much."

"How do you think I feel?"

He sighed. "Probably the same."

She had never met a man — or *anybody* — so quick to look at themselves like him. He was kind and reasonable, and whenever he went too far, he recognized it and adjusted, came at the project with a new perspective.

"I hope our son is like you," she said.

"If we have one, maybe he will be."

"You still don't believe I'm pregnant?"

"No, I do. I just think it will be a little girl. Strong and beautiful like her mother. A joy to bring into a world that is sadly short on it."

He had gotten a text from Ian. Left with a bright smile on his face to go play with fire. She took off soon after.

Two trips to the bank, and it was starting to get dark. One more so she could see what the route might look like in the morning in lower light. Slow and steady. Following the laws and signs and holding on so tight, her shoulders were knotting up.

She wasn't sure if she was imagining the smell of coffee when she passed Rush to Town — a name she loved in spite of all the scorn the others heaped on it — or if it was coming through the windows as she drove by. If she wasn't part of a ... she wasn't sure *what* to call it. A heist? Rescue mission?

If not for whatever it was, she would stop for the tallest coffee with all the caramel and whipped cream that would fit in the biggest cup they made.

Instead of driving along the front of the bank, she turned down the alley that ran along the side. As she passed the huge dumpsters, she wondered why a bank would even need them. Maybe it was part of the construction across the street. Or maybe it was for a planned project once it moved over.

She wasn't sure, but she was glad to see them angled

out in such a way that she could hook one with the front bumper. Move it to take up most of the alley. Block off the route to keep the bank isolated.

Left along the rear of the bank. Another left when that alley ended. After a few blocks, and she wasn't back on the street she had become familiar with the last two times, she regretted her decision. Everything suddenly looked different in the twilight.

Even as she tried to remain calm, panic began building. It was a small town — built like a grid — but she couldn't help feeling like it was expanding around her.

She had to turn around. Just pick a driveway or a parking lot.

No. She had to keep going until she saw something familiar. Make turns based on logic.

She rolled her eyes. It wasn't like she was caught in a maze.

She and Mo used to take off to drive down the back roads looking for property. Just pick a direction and try to spot real estate signs. No directions or GPS. No matter where they went, they always ended up finding something they knew. A road that took them toward home. A flea market. Something that jogged the memory.

"Oh, I know where I am now."

She bit back her rising anxiety. Reached for her braid, and when she didn't find it, she let out a strong, "Moth-erfucker!"

Now the fear was replaced by anger. She wasn't sure if it cleared her vision or just distracted her, but there was the weird angled intersection a mile up from the motel. She just didn't recognize it coming from this side.

She should have just stuck with her original route.

It was darkening into dusk when she pulled into the

spot in front of the room. She almost had to pry her own fingers free, and the relief at being back to familiarity and safety was enough to leave her chilled.

Now that she finally had something to do, she wasn't so sure anymore, but it was too late to back out now.

Chapter Fifteen

Ian had no worries. Felt like a feather as he skipped across the road to his room on the end. A bigger fleabag than even the piece of shit behind him. It had bigger rooms on either end. Two beds and a full kitchen.

He and his team could stay together. Mohammed always slept in a chair. That gave him a bed, and Shawna the other. He wished the arrangements could be a little different.

A thought he had been having lately. Shawna was coming out of her shell. Probably returning to the woman she had been before her terrible experience with ... Miguel. Even thinking the man's name made him sneer in disgust.

Having a job so personal. With such ramifications for defenseless children. It not only preyed on her emotions but his as well. Even Mohammed — a usually terse and seemingly unfeeling man — had become moody with the possible consequences of failure.

She was pulling closer to the confident woman she had been, and Ian's eyes were opening up to the possibilities.

Maybe take a break. Send Mohommed off with the physical copy of the evidence to accompany Gustoff and her bear as they found Mallory Black without getting killed by whoever was surely watching her too.

While he was gone … a fantasy he had trouble taking seriously. But maybe he could tell her how he felt. And she would feel the same way about him. And the rest would be whatever the rest could be.

He passed by the big truck Stan's trained bear drove. He had been so hesitant to let anyone know where he was staying. Ian understood. He was just trying to keep his lady safe.

A lady he really only just met, but to each his own.

It was funny when he had discovered Ian already knew where he was. Parked at the same hotel at which he and his team stayed. Haggis had been near speechless when he found out Stan and company were right across the street the whole time.

Ian skipped up to his room. Knocked twice. Waited a count of two and knocked two more times. Unlocked the door and entered to find Shawna and Mohammed at the table. Wires trailing in every direction. The glow of their monitors making their faces float above their dark uniforms like ghostly spirits summoned by the candlelight of a séance.

They looked at him, but only Shawna smiled. Instead of looking away with a flush of embarrassment, she held his gaze until he smiled back.

That fantasy was becoming more real by the moment.

His phone buzzed. He pulled it out, sad that he couldn't look at her smile anymore. Relieved that he wasn't standing under her scrutiny anymore.

His GPS tracker sent him a notification. When he opened it, he saw the package he was expecting coming toward the door. He held his hand up and brought his phone to the door, watching the dot approach. Looked through the eyepiece of his door at the courier walking up from a yellow Penske van.

The box he carried dangled on his hip. Ian knew he would handle it a little more carefully if he knew what was in it. Enough parts and explosives for two bombs. One large and one small.

Mohammed hustled over. Two pistols drawn and ready as he pushed into the corner next to the door hinges.

Ian pulled his own pistol. Slid his phone in his pocket. He put the barrel against the door. Aiming it through the thin wood at the young man reaching up to knock. A couple inches of pale belly showed when his dirty t-shirt rode up.

Ian opened the door enough to see outside. "Yeah."

"Just dropping off a box."

"Then drop it off."

The courier was young enough to be offended by everything but old enough to know when it was best to keep quiet about it. He shrugged. Bent to put the box on the stoop. "Whatever, man."

His hair flopped in his face. When he stood up his face had turned scarlet from exertion. He widened his eyes. Blew out a sigh that smelled like beer.

He seemed to wait to catch his balance, then he turned to go back to his truck.

"Yo," Ian shouted.

The kid turned back with his shoulder falling in a slump. "What, man. I gotta truck full of shit."

Ian reached out with a twenty dollar bill.

The kid's face lit up like somebody had opened a box of doughnuts. "Hey, cool!"

He snatched it from Ian's hand so fast it could have lit a

match. If he moved as fast as he did getting back to the truck the rest of the time, that belly might not protrude quite so much.

Ian pulled the box in. Nodded to Mohammed as he closed the door. Tossed the box up on the near bed. "Let's see what we have."

It was packed like he expected. Hardly anything to protect the contents. Mohammed chuckled as he went back to his computer.

Ian pulled everything out. Made sure everything was there, but at the bottom, he found something extra. A thermos, like something a construction worker would take to the job site. Big enough to hold a small bomb, just enough to throw a van into the street.

He sat with his own laptop and opened the program that monitored the radio bursts from the competitor's van. Masked signals in bursts to hide their communications as construction chatter. Sat there listening.

So blatantly obvious that even a contractor half as good as Ian would have seen it. They could listen all they wanted. He had every signal on his end covered. In the morning, he would jam them, running their signal through his equipment to make it look like they were still alive. Then he would blow the van.

They wouldn't know what hit them.

He texted Mo and set the Thermos next to his Wi-Fi inspector disguise. The finishing touches to what he was going to be wearing tomorrow.

Good planning led to good execution. Only he didn't have the reputation of being good. He was known for being the best.

Chapter Sixteen

The morning came so fast, then came to such a screeching halt, Ronnie thought it was going to give her whiplash.

Everybody had a job but her. She knew it was her fault for the way she had complained and demanded. Then went back on her word.

Gen had left without saying goodbye. Ronnie had gone next door to find it empty. Of course they were gone too. They were with Stan. Or Mo was with Haggis, and Gen was with Stan.

Jeanette was in her room waiting like her. Maybe she could cross the road and sit with her. She only really knew her for when she had pulled a gun on them in the restroom in Key West. Maybe that wasn't the best idea.

Shawna and Mohammed were finishing the evidence packets. All that was left was the addition of whatever Stan was getting at the bank. Then they would give one to Jeanette and one to her.

Then they would be off to have their fun.

She couldn't really call it fun though. She had no idea what their jobs really entailed, but if it was the same kind of thing they'd been doing with Stan, it probably wasn't fun at all.

Her world had shrunk to the three people she now loved as much as any family she had ever had. And now Stan had asked her to marry him. She was afraid he had only done it to keep her quiet.

She wondered if he knew something that she didn't, if he was lying about their chances at the bank today. Was she going to find out that she now alone?

She growled as she stood up. She walked to the door, but she knew she couldn't go anywhere. She stood out. Maybe she should have cut her hair like Gen had. Then there would be nothing to hide her face behind.

Maybe that was a good thing, though she noticed nobody asked her to cut it. They probably wanted her to hide it too. They probably couldn't stand looking at it either.

She rolled her eyes. "That's silly, girl."

Her voice sounded rougher than usual today. A lot of crying recently. The inside of her throat and lungs had been burned by the blast that scarred her face. It had taken months before she could make more than a whisper. Years before she could produce any volume.

It worked fine after so long, but it still sounded like a squeaky window fell on a dying frog.

She made a fourth cup of coffee. Pulled her chair to the window and drew the curtain back enough to see across the parking lot. Cars whizzed by, more than usual, but she hadn't paid attention this early in the morning. People going to work, or maybe just running the hell away from this shitty little town.

She blew on her coffee before taking a sip. Burned her tongue anyway.

A small pickup drove by, pulling into a spot at the end.

She watched a couple get out. Luggage the man pulled from the bed was dominated by a huge diaper bag. The woman carried a baby seat on her hip.

She thought of Gen and wondered if she would get the chance to see the baby she knew was coming. To smell the new skin of its head. Hold it to her so it could hear her heartbeat.

Maybe make Stan hold it so he could get used to the idea. Maybe talk about having one of their own.

The sun made everything scream with brightness. It was hard to believe that any bad things could happen under such a piercing spotlight.

The couple disappeared in a room several doors down.

Stan was probably already in the bank. It wouldn't be long now.

She looked down at the cooling coffee, decided to pour it out and switch to water.

When she looked up, she saw the rear bumper of a black car drive by. She pushed her face against the window so she could see it as it angled away, but she couldn't tell if it was a Dodge.

She was bad with cars. Stan could name the make, model, and year of everything on the road. It was a *guy* thing. Sometimes frustrating.

Remember what kind of engine was in a certain type of Ford, but his anniversary slipped his mind.

She let the curtain fall closed as she got up to set her cup on the counter.

She washed her face for the third time and put her moisturizer on, paying particular attention to the scars from her most recent surgery. She put her mask on. Colored to look like her skin, it hid the pale grafts and protected the long healing process. One of these days — if they ever stopped operating on her — she could finally live without it.

She sat back down. Another black car on the road going the other way. Or was it the same car? Pulled out of the parking lot and driving off.

The stress of waiting. Of boredom. She was seeing things. When she heard a car door shut, she sat up with a jolt.

It was the young father at his pickup. She relaxed back into her chair. Reached for a coffee cup that was no longer there.

She could just make out the doors on the units across the road. Haggis' truck sitting high and proud. A small dark car sitting in its shadow. Was it black? One of those Dodges?

And there was a white van next to it. Like Ian's.

She rolled her eyes. Everywhere she looked there were bad guys. Even when there weren't.

She stood with a nervous chuckle. Centered herself in the space between the door and the bed, ran through several stretches, and looked back through the window.

The young lovers' pickup was still there. Haggis' truck. The van. The black car was gone, but she didn't see it anywhere else.

She moved away from the window, feeling ridiculous. Watching the parking lot wasn't going to make time move faster. It was just hard sitting around waiting for her world to come back.

Chapter Seventeen

Mo hopped out of the small SUV. Haggis swung around to climb up the ramp into the parking garage. The morning was dark, and with the power off on the line of buildings across the street from the bank, it felt like he was walking into a void.

Like a hole into space had opened, and he was about to get sucked into it.

For fun, he tried the front door. It was locked. The lobby lights in the bank cast an expanding triangle of light on the sidewalk behind him that he could see in the reflection of the surplus store window.

Not quite enough light to make him feel like he wasn't floating away.

He walked to the corner, past the side door facing the parking garage. The overnight lights lit the side of the building up enough that anybody driving by would see him trying to pick the lock.

He continued on to the back, into the weedy alley to the back door shielded by a fence. He swung his backpack down and pulled the lock-picking gun out. He installed the bump rod and inserted it into the lock in the rusty metal door, holding it steady while he put the torsion wrench in. Put gentle pressure on it as he pulled the trigger in quick succession. On the fourth pull, the lock turned.

He dropped the lock pick gun back into the pack. Opened the door and stepped into the musty dark. He turned on the small penlight he had clipped to the zipper of the backpack. Keeping the light almost completely shielded, he looked at the stacks of old clothes and broken cardboard boxes. More shelves of stock the light couldn't reach.

A small doorway led him deeper into a small hallway lined with more military surplus, then into the rear of the storeroom. The light from the bank was enough to see where he was going between the circular racks. He ducked from the headlight beam that swept by as a car passed and pulled into the bank parking. He had no way of knowing if it was an employee or customer.

He looked at his watch. A little past 7 in the morning Definitely an employee. Maybe even Mr. Clarke himself.

He busied himself with the task of setting a charge that would blow the concrete columns out. The blast radius extending to the front wall. The front windows and door would explode into the street. The supports would collapse, and when the second floor fell, the smoke and dust would roll out to fill the air for blocks.

He finished with one side. Dodged more headlights as he made his way to the other one. He felt that old adrenaline from the Army. Setting a charge on the door. Waiting for the moment of detonation. Heart pounding and eyes wide.

When he was finished, the sky was filling with light. It was well past 8. Stan and Gen would be in the alley soon. He only had a little bit of time to get it ready.

He clapped his hands. No problem.

A couple hundred feet of det cord, held on in a concentric circle to the face of the columns using black duct tape. The tails trailing down to meet between them on the floor. He tied them into the blasting switch that would provide the current that would set them off.

Then a small patty of C4 in the center of each duct tape spiderweb. The pressure wave from the det cord was more than enough to provide ignition. Less than a quarter pound total, but enough to turn most of the visible concrete into dust.

The shock wave would blow the det cord fire out, so they wouldn't burn the whole town down. He just had to hook the receiver up to the blasting switch, then arm the system before fucking off.

It was only a few minutes before 9. Half of the bank parking lot was already full. No Dodge Charger, but that didn't mean nobody was in there waiting.

He picked up his backpack, much lighter now that it was mostly empty. Back into the rear alley to walk away from the street in front of the parking garage past the building under construction.

Jogging was so much easier these days now that he was so much lighter, but it was still several blocks down. Up a side street to the alley that led behind the Rush to Town. He finally saw the Subaru behind the bank, across from the dumpsters in the shadow of a white building. He couldn't remember if it was a dentist or an insurance office. Plenty of parking in the empty lot, making the little blue hatchback stand out. Couldn't Ian have picked something a little more discreet?

He saw a flash of blonde hair through the window, then Gen climbed out. Rushed up to throw herself into his arms. He carried her back to the car. Set her down so she could climb into the back seat. The driver's seat was electronic, and it seemed to take forever for the motors to move it all the way back. He still had to cram himself in.

Maybe he should have let Gen stay behind the wheel.

As soon as he got settled, he handed the wireless detonator to Stan. He took it like it was a live snake, a tiny cylinder the size of a personal flashlight. One click of the button charged it up to send the signal. The second click made the magic happen.

Stan slid it into his inside pocket before getting out. He still looked like a retired party clown that liked to scare children, but his suit was pretty sharp. Overdressed, but what else do you wear when trying to get your safety deposit box back from criminals?

Without a word, Stan got out.

He walked across the alley. Hugged the wall on his way to the street. A little unsteady as he disappeared around the corner.

"Is he limping?"

Gen leaned up to put her head between the front seats. "He's got a bone spur that's giving him trouble. He needs another surgery. Been putting it off, but he's been on his feet a lot lately."

"Foot," Mo said.

"What?"

"He only has one foot."

She leaned back in confusion. "He has two feet, just one is fake."

Mo straightened in realization. "Oh yeah. I guess you're right."

She looked out the window. "How long do you think it will be?"

"I have no idea, but I can't imagine it being very long."

"Do we have a plan B?"

"Nope."

"Should we?"

"Probably."

"Are we going to be okay?"

"I think so."

She nodded. Chewed on a nail. "Will it be very long?"

"You already asked that."

"Oh." She threw herself back in her seat, and the car rocked with a squeak of springs. "Will it be big?"

He grinned at her through the mirror. "Oh yeah."

Probably too big, if he was going to be honest with himself. But this might be the last time he was in a position to blow something up with intent.

Or the last day he would be alive.

Might as well go out with a bang.

Chapter Eighteen

Haggis parked the SUV on the first layer of the parking garage. No attendants. No signs prohibiting parking. Only a warning against remaining overnight.

He felt more alive than he had in years. More purposeful. Effort felt good again. And the result was going to be satisfying.

Not to mention what was waiting for him when he got done.

He shook his head as he climbed the stairs to the third level. How had he gotten so lucky? To just fall into something so beautiful so late in life. Love. And he thought he was correct in calling how he felt for Jeanette *love*.

He hated leaving her behind. But Ian's people were competent. She was supposed to go to their room to get her collection of evidence back. Once they added in the extra stuff from the deposit box, she would keep it until she could get it back to Mallory Black. If the spam server worked like they claimed, she could be more vocal about her efforts to bring this case to light. Maybe she could even be the official face of the whole thing.

From the stories Jeanette had told him about her, she might need a little public redemption.

He got to the third floor and held the strap on his shoulder as he walked across the empty platform. Straight to his hidey-hole. He smiled at the excitement swelling in his chest.

He had loved designing and building prosthetics, but the monotony of it — or at least that feeling of punching a clock — had started to wear on him. Nothing like his job in the Corps.

But so little was.

The constant stress had made him leave, and he had been searching for a replacement ever since.

After squeezing into the opening, he was able to slide his pack off. He crouched down to open it up. A protein bar. Canteen of water with an electrolyte packet dissolved into it, like salty lemonade. And at the bottom was the rifle. His ol' girl.

She had been with him for a long time. Didn't mind being in the dark as long as she could come out every now and again for some real work. This was her day.

He assembled the rifle with muscle memory. No need to look. Had her up on his shoulder in minutes.

Through the fluttering leaves of the tree outside the railing, he saw the front door of the bank. Swaying with his breath until he tightened up and blew his air out. The view steadied. Held still for the moments he would need to fire.

He drew back with a grin. Inserted the magazine and chambered a round. Sighted down again. Kept his finger off the trigger as he lined up one more time. At this angle there was no chance of a miss going into the lobby. Or a round travelling through the target and striking somebody behind.

His spot was perfect.

He sat back with the butt of the rifle between his knees. Thought about what it was going to feel like if he actually got to squeeze off a few and wondered if he would get caught. Somebody coming up on him and filling the alcove with lead.

He shrugged. If this was his last day on earth, so what? It'd been a good run. And that's why he was so satisfied. The last few days had been some of the best.

He did good work at Ossi-Pro — helped a lot of people — but something about this seemed a little more important. Saving children. Making Jeanette smile.

He checked his watch. It was close. He stepped through the narrow gap. Leaned against the railing to sight down the street. Couldn't quite get the angle. Had to lean a little too far out, straining his abs to hold him up.

More traffic than there had been. Activity at the construction site.

He laughed in surprise when he saw Mo. Jogging across the street to disappear behind the coffee shop. His empty backpack bounced on his shoulders like it was trying to escape.

Haggis pulled himself back in and set up his working position. Small green hand towel on the rail. One knee planted. The other one at ninety degrees. Relaxed spine and shoulders.

When he set his gaze through the scope, he wasn't surprised to see the front door centered in his field of view. His body knew what to do without him directing his thoughts toward the action.

Habit and repetition.

Staring at a target always made him wonder. What would his life have been like without the war and killing? The depression and loneliness. The empty beds and long nights staring into the dark.

Was he who he would have been without it? Would he have been better or worse? It was an interesting question to him. One he would never get answered, but he couldn't help asking.

Would Jeanette have liked that other Haggis? Would that other Haggis have liked her? What was it about them that had drawn them so close so quickly?

He knew part of it was the shared experience of killing her attackers in her hotel room. Whatever gap that had still existed between them was closed when they were thrown together fighting for their lives.

Then he was gripped by a cold thought. What if she died today? What if he had to go on without her? Though it felt like they had been together for years already, he barely knew her. Would he get over it? Would saving those girls be worth never knowing what would have been?

Sweat sprang out between his shoulder blades. What if they had missed something? Men breaking down her door at this very moment. What would they do to her? What would he be walking into when he was finished?

He wasn't sure if he could handle seeing her broken.

There had been plenty of women in his life, but no love. He had just accepted the fact that so many missions that ended in a kill and a pat on the back for a job well done had rendered him unable to feel it. A numb, empty shell.

Flitting from one thing to the next — one woman to another — like a butterfly looking for just the right flower.

Getting bored with a job. Wishing he was back behind the scope, even while knowing one more mission would kill him. Or change him for good.

Looking in the mirror and being afraid that he would never be better. Or normal.

And meeting Jeanette had changed all that. He had

been so surprised by it he had been unable to look at it with the right perspective. Shock and incredulity, and finally a resigned acceptance. Why shouldn't it be the way he finally found what he'd been looking for all his life?

He nodded to himself. Reset his posture. Got his breathing back under control.

He had done bad things, but he wasn't a bad man. Jeanette thought she was a bad person, but he knew better. The proof was that they had found each other. Both of them in a despair so deep, neither of them even knew they were in the hole.

When you stopped trying to climb out, you stopped seeing the walls around you.

No. He knew things were going to be all right because he wanted them to be. He had never asked for anything. Never wished things to be different. Except for now. He would will it into existence. He would believe it, therefore it would happen.

Movement at the top of his view brought him focus. He scanned up to see Stan's limo around the corner. Looked around like he was expecting to see an old friend. Haggis tracked his movement with his reticle barely deviating from the center of his head.

Stan went inside, and Haggis began a steady search of the area. More traffic, a few pedestrians, but nobody followed Stan into the bank.

Haggis wiped his eyes. Stared at the moisture his tears had caused. Set himself back under his rifle. Thumbed off the safety.

Even with all the pain, he *still* had to admit — it had been a good run.

Haggis suddenly realized why he was ready to die. Because he was ready to kill again.

Chapter Nineteen

There was no lobby in the bank. Just doors that opened onto a big room. Intricate tile floor, polished wood paneling, granite counters and desktops.

They kept it cold inside. Stan looked up at the complicated arches and beams. Lazy fans spinning to wash fresh air across the winding line created by brass posts and red velvet ropes.

There were no guards present, at least none visible.

Hushed activity in the background. Quiet voices. Shuffling papers. Plastic keyboards instead of what his mind expected.

Clacking metal and the ding of return bells from period typewriters.

Except for the monitors hanging on the walls running videos about the service offered by the Belling National trust, it would have felt like stepping back in time.

His footsteps echoed as he approached the counter. The left one louder than the right as his limp got worse. The stabbing ache of his stump in the bottom of the socket had been a nagging complaint in the background, but he must not have gotten it seated right this morning. Or something was down in there.

If they made it through the day, he would have to do something about it. Maybe Haggis could work up something so he could avoid another surgery.

He smiled at the young woman waiting to help him. Her return smile was cold yet polite. "How may I help you this morning, sir?"

"I'm here to see Mr. Clarke, please."

Her smile decreased by a degree. "I'm sorry, but his time is by appointment only."

"Is it? That's funny, the last time I was on the phone, he told me to just come in whenever I wanted."

Her smile was slowly morphing into a sneer. "Policy has changed."

"What if it was *really* important?"

"If you would like to make an appointment, I can take your information."

Stan matched her expression. "That would be very accommodating." He reached into his pocket. Fingers moving past the detonator to a business card. It had his assumed name printed on it and a phone number to an answering service.

When she looked at the card and saw his name, her face froze. She made a show of looking at the time. "Actually, I believe he might be free at the moment. Let me check for you."

Without waiting for him to respond, she spun away. The echoes of her heels striking the cold floor were like distant gunfire.

He looked at the desks behind the counter. Busy workers already deep into their tasks. Only they kept looking up at him from the corners of their eyes.

Something about them ... the set of their shoulders. The furtive glances. They were scared.

Stan felt doubt creep into his confidence like a wedge.

What would it take to keep the bank open during the renovation of Old Downtown? Ian's story about the construction worker waiting for city services that weren't coming. The military surplus store owner angry because he had to wait for his power to come back on because the bank was a holdout for some reason.

Puzzle pieces Stan couldn't quite fit together.

"Mr. Franklin?" The voice pulled Stan from his thoughts. He had only ever met Clarke on the phone. He turned to meet him, but was surprised when he looked nothing like his expectations. Instead of the large man his voice sounded like, he looked like one of the officers on the Death Star. Gray and gaunt. Powerful hands sticking out of spindly sleeves. Thinning hair greased down and slicked back. "It's so good to finally meet you in person," Clarke said.

His grip was like oily iron. "Likewise," Stan said.

Clarke glanced back at the woman that had taken Stan's card. He pulled his jacket straight. "Would you like some coffee?"

"Oh, no thank you. In fact, I think it best if we just move straight to the business at hand."

His smile looked like he was sick to his stomach but struggling to be polite. "Of course." He held his hand up to point at the rear corner. "If we could just ..."

Stan nodded, and moved in the direction indicated. Clarke rushed to get alongside him, but the woman remained a few steps behind.

"I must apologize," Clarke said. "The construction has been moving more slowly than we had anticipated."

That doubt rose up again. Stan tried to pinpoint the

source, but Clarke continued, "I've had a particularly difficult financial matter keeping me busy."

Stan understood him to be talking about the office sending assholes to give him shit about the safety deposit box contents.

"It's had my wife worried about the long hours. She's very protective of me."

They had even threatened his wife.

"But once it is resolved, things will be back to normal."

They told him to cooperate, and they would go away.

Stan nodded. "I understand. And I *hope* things get back to normal. Life is so uncertain sometimes."

Don't bet on it. These people lie.

"I expect you are correct, Mr. Franklin."

It sounded like he already suspected they were lying.

Through a doorway in the corner. Down a wide hallway that turned at the end. He thought they were probably parallel with the dumpsters outside. He didn't know if there was another hall that led to a different part of the bank. To a rear door. He would have to get back out the front.

They turned left at the end of the hallway. Decorative stairs went to the lower level. A room lined with little locked doors.

"You know," Stan said. "When you were first recommended to me, I was in the need of a general service. I must say, you have far exceeded the initial request."

Clarke covered his heart with both hands. "That makes me proud, sir. Steady clients like you are difficult to maintain."

Stan thought about the woman behind them. Quietly following. Why was Clarke still speaking in code? Was there a listening device nearby, or …

He decided to drop some of the pretense. "They either get killed or stop paying, don't they?"

Clarke looked at him in surprise. Then he recovered with a nod. "That is precisely correct."

He indicated a wide table in the center of the room. "I'll only be a moment."

Clarke walked to the bank of doors on the front wall. A row slightly bigger than the rest. As he released the first drawer, Stan heard another set of footprints descend the stairs. When he turned around, he wasn't surprised to see an armed man jogging to the bottom. The woman from behind the counter holding a pistol aimed at his face threw him a little though.

Then he got it. It wasn't the city that was keeping the bank open against the wishes of the nearby business owners. It was Hemingway's office. Whoever the organization was that wanted the evidence.

He kept his hands still at his side and met the woman's smug gaze. "So … you just threaten the City Council? Like you did to Clarke? Let us sit in the back for a week or two, or we'll kill your kids?"

She nodded as her partner came alongside her. "That is almost exactly right."

He shook his head. "What kind of kinky shit are you into to be a part of this shit? Who did you rape?"

Her smile tightened. "None of your business."

Her partner snickered. "She fucked almost every one of her students."

"And you fucked corpses," she snapped.

He shrugged. "To each his own. But I like kids too."

Mr. Clarke cleared his throat. "Do you have your keys, sir?"

Stan held his hands up. "I do."

Teacher nodded. "Good." She extended her other hand. "Give 'em over, please."

Gravedigger held his gun steady as Stan reached into his front pocket. Handed her the keys. She nodded as she took them. "Now open the jacket."

"I'm not armed," Stan said, but he complied. Holding it wide and lifting it off his belt. Turning around.

"I gotta admit," Gravedigger said. "You look different. I didn't recognize you."

"Running's been hard on us all."

Teacher sighed. "It's a disguise, you imbecile."

Stan rolled his eyes. "Can we get on with it?"

She smiled. "So eager. Fine."

Gracedigger hopped over to grab Stan by the collar. Drug him over to the wall to sling him into a chair. His head rapped off the wall, but he managed to keep from falling to the floor.

He shook his head as he straightened. That's why nobody was outside. They were already in here waiting. They knew he was coming. Knew they were all here. Just waiting to strike until he got the boxes opened.

He had no way of warning anybody.

Clarke presented the boxes and stepped back. He sent a look of apology over Teacher's shoulder. Stan held his hand up and shook his head. There was no need for Clarke to blame himself. He was caught in the same trap as Stan.

Teacher opened the first box. A little bigger than the large briefcase inside it. She glanced back over her shoulder. "Is this locked?"

Stan shook his head. When she turned back to open it, Gravedigger looked back. Up on his tiptoes to see what was inside.

Stan grabbed the detonator. Switched it to his left

hand. Clicked the button once to arm it. It sounded like an old camera's flash charging up.

"We got it," Teacher said.

Gravedigger dropped back onto his heels. "Open the other one."

Teacher shook her head. "We got what we need."

"But there might be something cool in it."

She sighed, but before she could respond, Stan teased, "Go ahead. It might be worth your while."

"Fine."

They opened the other one, and Stan knew they'd find a case much like the first. Heard the latches click. Now for the part where the case became different. He heard them both catch their breaths.

"How much is that?" Gravedigger whispered.

Stan worked his left foot up the right pant leg to hit the pressure relief valve on his socket. The vacuum broke, and air hissed in to let his stump come free. "A million dollars to the penny," he said.

Gravedigger was too busy staring at the money to notice him reaching for the Everyday Carry, but Teacher did. Bringing her gun up and opening her mouth to tell him not to move.

Before she made it all the way around, Stan hit the button again.

Chapter Twenty

Ian pulled his van into the same spot he had parked in the other day. Right next to the air handlers. Metal cubes that looked like they were growing out of the ground, like eggs that would one day hatch into a new building.

Many of the other spaces were filled with various trucks and vans. All manly vehicles, the kind that did the hard jobs. Including the other white van sitting on the street, right where it had been the whole time.

Ian opened the laptop on the center console. Checked the signals coming from his competitor. Isolated them. Repeated them. Jammed them.

Now they were just talking to themselves.

He was already in his construction worker disguise. Roll of paper. Lunch box and thermos held against his chest. He got out and closed the door with his hip.

He almost started whistling as he walked to the sidewalk. Glanced at the van's rearview mirror, saw nobody in the driver's seat. Must be in the back. In the middle of their screens and gadgets. Like a funnel spider crawling back to stay out of the light.

When he was even with the rear bumper. He pretended to trip. Juggled the lunchbox and thermos. Dropped the blueprints.

When he went down to his knees, he set the thermos over the curb into the street. Just in front of the rear tire. Grabbed his roll of paper and the lunchbox. Stood up with an embarrassed smile and a shake of his head.

He continued along the sidewalk to the front of the end of the scaffolding. Ducked behind it to go inside.

Like the last time, he nodded and waved, smiled at anybody that looked his way.

Right back out to the parking lot and straight to his van. He jumped inside. Crawled into the back, pulling his laptop to join the rest of his equipment. Checked out the radio bursts from the other van. Still blasting. Completely unaware that their branches had been pruned.

He checked the time. Only a few minutes past 9. He readied his own detonator and waited for Mo's explosion, hoping it was big enough for him to hear it.

The other van's transmission was steady. An uninterrupted stream. He stared at it, counting under his breath. Just before he got to 200, a tremendous explosion split the silence.

The van rocked a split-second after he cried out in surprise. He looked out the window, expecting to see a black cloud rushing by, but except for a bit of rolling debris, the explosion had been all bark.

He turned back to his screens. Hit his detonator before the rumble from the first explosion was gone.

His thermos exploded with a much less dramatic sound. Like a shotgun blast. Then the rattling crash of the van landing on its side.

He clapped his hands. Realized he hadn't bothered to watch if the street had been clear of traffic. Then he giggled like an excited child. He imagined the van tipped into the street. Leaning on a Ford Escort with a burning clutch as the driver tried to get away.

When he looked, he could just see the rear wheel of the van past the corner of the building under construction. A piece of scaffolding fell to the sidewalk. A clatter that preceded the panicked exodus of the workers from inside.

They ran into the street and stared around with wide eyes. A few of them headed to their vehicles. Ian figured he should head out before a bottleneck grew in the entrance to the parking lot. Or people coming into Old Downtown found the road blocked and started using the lot to turn around in.

He turned to shut down his equipment. Paused in confusion when he saw the data stream from the other van. Still broadcasting, like nothing had happened. How was it still going?

He left everything running as he got out. Left his door open. Pushed past a couple of workers. The van had landed perfectly across both lanes. A tiny bit of space on either side that a motivated motorist could use to get by.

Fluids leaking. A chunk of curb blown away.

He stumbled into the street. Put his face to the window on the rear doors. Tinted as dark as paint, so he couldn't see inside.

He heard the crack of a shot in the distance. A scream. Three more shots. Spaced and measured.

He turned from the van. Confusion rising to panic. He jumped back up on the sidewalk and grabbed the metal tube that had fallen off the scaffolding.

Whipped back around, dodged another worker on his way to the parking lot. Lunged at the van and sent the tube through the van window. Cleared out the fragments on the edges before looking inside.

There was nobody inside. Just a black case. A wire running from a hole next to hinge up to the dash. Likely a power source. But for what?

He reeled back in horror. A car already blocked the parking lot entrance. Trucks and vans backed up, waiting for their turn to get out.

Ian ran back to his van and jumped in to look at the screen of his laptop. The steady line of data coming from behind him. Just a meaningless signal set to repeat. Bait for somebody who thought they were better than they were.

He scrambled into the front seat with a cry of horror. Mohammed and Shawna didn't know what was coming. He snatched up his phone and got into the driver's seat. Called the room phone. It rang and rang. Maybe they did know what was coming. Because it was already there.

He started the engine. Looked at the people and vehicles forming a jam behind him. Frantic to find a way out, he looked at the fence separating him from the manicured lawn of the business in front of him. An optometrist? Fucking day care?

It didn't matter. He put it in reverse and backed up for a little room. Slammed it into drive, smashed the gas, and held on as he threw gravel over the protesting workers behind him. Shot forward and smashed through the fence in a jolt of sparks and screaming metal.

The van tore through the hedge to hit the dark asphalt of the driveway. He glanced the passenger side off a tree, tearing the side mirror away. Drifted into the street with a section of chain link bouncing behind him. He hit the corner to cut off a red Suburban as he aimed for the center of town. The fencing flew from his bumper to spread out in the air like a sheet of spider web.

Traffic became heavier as he neared the roundabout at the town square. Sirens swelled in the distance. He forced himself to take his turn in the circle. When he realized he was repeating her name — "Shawna, Shawna, Shawna, Shawna …" — he bit his lip until he tasted blood.

How had he missed it?

Because he was overconfident.

How had they beaten him?

Because he was blind.

How could he have let this happen?

So sure that he had it under control, he hadn't bothered to double-check. He hadn't entertained the thought that he should be a little more careful just in case they were better than him.

But they weren't. They hadn't beaten him. He had beaten himself.

He screamed at the windshield, pleading with the cars to get out of his way and begging for her to be alive.

He promised himself that he would tell her. If she had survived what he feared had come for her … he would tell her he loved her. He would finally tell her how proud he was. How good a job she was doing. How he wanted nothing more in the world than her.

Red and blue lights ahead. The blare of air horns. Shrieking sirens. They were coming his way in an open lane so he didn't bother slowing down or getting over. He flinched away from the sound as they blew by, but he held the van steady. He had an emergency too.

Chapter Twenty-One

Jeanette was packed and ready. Not like it had taken much. She had so few belongings with her. A trip that had taken much longer than she expected, and she never bought anything more to help with the extended stay. The same three pairs of jeans. Everything else rotating through washings that were making them all gray and threadbare.

Threads in her bras starting to fray.

She was supposed to go over to the room on the end. Pick up the evidence after they got back from the bank, but she was nervous and lonely. She missed Haggis. Pushed down the indigestion that came from anxiety. A growing fear that he wouldn't come back.

And she was ready for it if that's what was going to happen. She was a part of this thing now, dragged into it by Mallory Black.

She felt for the wad of cash in her fanny pack. At least she hadn't taken it free of charge like she usually did. Plenty of money left for some new bras and t-shirts.

It was barely light out. Not even close to the time when everybody should be coming back. No reason to sit alone.

That guy Ian worked with – the one who had told her to call him Jihad – scared the shit out of her.

Not because she thought he was going to be violent toward her, but because she couldn't read his eyes. They were dead no matter what he was doing or saying. Like he was being driven by an entity that didn't know what it was like to be human. Learning to operate the meat puppet by only reading the manual.

Shawna was nice though. Quiet and mousy, but Jeanette suspected there was some fire under all those quiet smiles and shy looks.

She slipped her jacket on and snapped her pistol into the holster. Stepped into the cool morning air for a deep breath before walking down the front of the motel to the last room.

Swallowed her uncertainty. Tapped on the door.

It was only a few seconds before it opened, swinging wide with nobody in front of it, like somebody was hiding behind it, ready to spring out for a nice scare.

"It's just me," she said. "Jeanette Gustoff."

"Get the fuck in already." Like the monster under the bed convincing a kid to let his foot dangle down, Jihad was talking to her from his hiding spot behind the door.

She jumped with a grunt of apology. Rushed inside and turned to keep her back to the wall as she shut the door. Put his own pistol away in a holster behind his back. "Clear," he shouted.

Shawna came out of the bathroom. Pistol held ready in both hands. She eased the hammer back down and put her pistol away the same as Jihad. Then she waved with a small smile. "Hi."

Jihad locked the door. Walked past her to sit back at the table. "We are just waiting for Ian to come back."

Jeanette nodded. "I was waiting too."

He hummed like somebody trying to figure out a riddle. "Then why are you here? They aren't back yet."

Jeanette shrugged. "I just didn't want to be alone."

He turned to look back at her over his shoulder, and she saw genuine emotion on his face for the first time. Curiosity. "And you wanted to be with *us*?"

She nodded. "Yeah. Why not?"

His eyes softened. "Thank you." He pointed to one of the empty chairs around the table. "Would you like to sit?"

It put her a little too close to him, but she felt like she was getting a dog to trust her enough to eat from her hand. "Sure," she said, walking over to sit without hesitation.

Shawna watched her with wide eyes. An expectant smile. "Nobody usually wants to be around us."

Jihad smiled. It looked like his spleen hurt. "We make people uncomfortable."

Jeanette forced a laugh. "They just don't know you."

"Do you?"

This time her laugh was genuine. "No, not really."

Jihad surprised her by joining her. Full and rich laughter that sounded at odds with what she was used to from him. It set Shawna off too. Looking across at Jihad in surprise. Eyes wide like a little kid discovering that fairies were real.

She leaned back, feeling better about her decision to come over early, and there was a knock on the door.

Jihad sobered so quickly, it was like the laughter was just a memory. Shawna tensed as Jihad got up and crept toward the door in a ready crouch.

The blast of a shotgun made her ears pound with pressure, and the door knob exploded into the room with a burst of wood and debris.

The door smashed open, and three men crowded in through a cloud of gunpowder smoke.

Jeanette jumped up to face the door, but Shawna grabbed her shoulder. Pulled her back with a strength so unexpected, Jeanette stumbled against the back wall and almost fell down.

She got her balance back, and Shawna pressed back into her with her arms spread. Like she was a mother hiding her child from an intruder.

Over her shoulder, Jeanette watched Jihad erupt into motion. So fast and fluid, she couldn't believe she was looking at the movements of a human.

Into the guard of the lead man to push the shotgun to the side. It fired again, and both pillows on the nearest bed blew apart into a chaos of shredded fabric and fluff.

Jihad drove his fist into the guy's throat. A choking sound and bugging eyes, and Jihad rotated out from under his reach to spin a kick up into the second man's head.

Shawna drew her pistol. Pushed Jeanette back into the wall as she braced to fire, hitting the lead man in the belly. Another shot in the chest. A third in his face. Blood filled the air behind him as he fell back into the second man reeling from Jihad's attack.

The third shotgun blast hit Shawna in the chest.

Shot tore the papers and wood. Crackled through the plastic of the computers. Screens shattered.

Jeanette felt the burning sting in her forearms. Saw blood soak the fabric of her sleeve.

Shawna's weight hit her, and she cried out from the fresh contact. Her gun trembled as she tried to aim again.

Jihad had one hand behind him. His other hand tangled in the shirt of the second man as he fell from the kick to his head. Mouth hanging open and eyes closed.

Jihad had his pistol out and halfway around him when the third man found himself clear as the second man pulled from Jihad's grip on his way to the floor.

The third man fired.

Blood exploded from Jihad's neck. He fired as he jerked back from the impact. The third guy took it in the belly. Staggered back as he fired two more times. Jihad's head snapped back as his scalp split apart in a burst of splattering bone and brain tissue.

Shawna pushed forward with a groan. Jeanette fell to the side. Looked up as Shawna opened fire. The lower part of her face was a mess of blood and torn skin. Ruined by the shotgun. Blood-soaked teeth gritted as she shot the third guy four times. He fell back against the jamb with his shirt front turning crimson from neck to waist. Crumpled into a heap, falling to stretch out onto the stoop.

The second guy pushed to his hands and knees, shaking his head.

Shawna fired, but the bullet missed, skipping off the concrete outside with a zing.

He rolled to bring his own gun up, and they fired at the same time. Shawna missed again, but he hit her in the belly, then the eye. Blood spread out behind her head like angel wings, and she slid down the wall to rest on Jeanette's legs.

She heard the guy get up. She pulled her gun. Saw the pregnant mother standing in front of her. Shook her head to banish the vision, but she still heard her cries. They got louder as she thumbed off the safety. By the time she tightened her grip and pushed to stand, she heard the scream of the baby too.

She could have killed them, and just the possibility of it had ruined her life. Even though she carried her pistol, she had sworn never to use it to shoot another human again.

As Shawna's blood soaked into her pant leg, she broke her promise. Pain exploded in her side as she twisted to fire. Kept squeezing until the gun was empty and the man was down.

Blood and smoke filled the air. She tried blinking it away, but it stayed there. She couldn't figure out why.

Three steps out from behind the table, and her legs gave way. She landed in a heap, and the pain in her side deepened into a searing heat. Her lap was filling with blood.

She looked out the front door. Back up to the table. Pulled herself to her feet. Stood there shaking until she got a deep breath.

Was that scream from outside? Voices. She saw somebody in the doorway. She screamed and pointed her gun at the shadow, and it raised its hands. Darted away. She nodded in satisfaction.

Scooped up the large envelopes off the table. They were waiting for that final bit of evidence Stan was bringing, but she had to get them to safety. She had to get out.

She held them to her chest and turned toward the door. Haggis' truck seemed so far away.

She stepped over the first dead man. Edged past the second one. Stumbled over Jihad. Finally made it to the door. Paused to catch her breath.

Blood trickled down her leg.

She looked up. A woman gasped and ducked back into her door. A young man that looked familiar stared at her as he spoke into a phone.

Jeanette took one last look behind her, but couldn't remember what she was looking for. Turned back and searched the parking lot until she saw Haggis' truck. It suddenly seemed farther away than before. She lowered her head and took another step.

Chapter Twenty-Two

When the explosion shook the bank, even Stan ducked at the sound and vibration. Thought Mo might be a little out of touch with current breaching techniques.

Clarke dropped to the floor, much more spry than his frail appearance would suggest. Gravedigger and Teacher both braced against the table. Dropped into a crouch and looked at each other in confusion.

Stan had a choice as he lifted his prosthesis and lunged forward with all the strength he could muster with just one leg.

Go for the beauty, or go for the beast.

Gravedigger saw him coming. Stepped in to meet him, and that was the deciding factor. Stan brought the Everyday Carry down across the bridge of Gravedigger's nose. Bone shattered, and blood sprayed to follow the arc of the fake foot as it ended its descent by crashing into the edge of the table and breaking free of the socket.

Teacher turned to react, but his momentum drove her back to fold over her side.

Gravedigger dropped his pistol in favor of catching the

flap of skin that used to be his nose as it slapped against his chin. Blood filling his palms like he was standing at a well pump.

Teacher rebounded to fall against Stan to drag him down to the floor. He dropped onto his back, and she landed on top of him, her left breast squashed against his face.

He thought about distracting her by biting it as hard as he could, but the thought evaporated when she fired the gun between them. A muffled burn, and heat traced along the inside of his thigh. Her second shot hit nothing but marble tile. She didn't get to fire a third because he went with his first thought. Opened his mouth and bit as hard as he could.

His mouth filled with blood, and her scream split his ears. She jerked back, and fabric and flesh tore. He sat up and shook his head. Her scream became frantic, and the thought of having a mouthful of somebody's body made his stomach heave.

He opened his teeth, and she fell back to swing her gun up, clipping him on the temple with the barrel. The cut she opened dripped into his eyes, and he blindly lunged for her throat. Her skin was too slick for him to get a good grip. He saw the shadowy arc of the gun coming for his face again. Let go with one hand to catch it before it could connect. Dug the thumb of his other hand into her trachea.

Teacher let go of the gun to grab his wrist with both hands. Wheezing desperate cries that sounded like a horse drowning in a trough. Just when she tore his hand free, he got the barrel of her pistol sunk into the flesh under her jaw. He fired, and the tip of her head opened to spray the bottom of the table.

Stan fell back to get his breath and wipe his eyes clear,

only to see Gravedigger raising his foot to stomp on his face. Stan jerked his head to the side, and Gravedigger's heel gouged a burning furrow along his scalp. Stan extended his arm to bury the gun in Gravedigger's balls. One round was all it took.

Gravedigger fell over with a scream that sounded like it should have come from his partner. High-pitched and squealing. Stan rolled out from under Teacher and climbed on top of a thrashing Gravedigger. He put one between his eyes to end it and turned to grab the edge of the table to pull himself up.

Clarke was already there. Closing and fastening both cases. Standing them up and sliding them to be within Stan's reach. "I'm terribly sorry about this, sir."

"It's not your fault. Don't worry about it."

"Thank you, sir. But I do need to ask a favor, please."

"What is it?"

"I suspect I will no longer benefit from your business. I will need a new client, but I need to maintain their prospective trust. Could you …"

"Shoot you?"

Clarke sagged in relief. "Yes, sir. Possibly somewhere that is not life-threatening?"

Stan reached across and put the barrel against the outside of Clarke's thin biceps. The shot took a chunk of flesh with it, but he suspected he would recover just fine.

Clarke slapped his hand over the wound, and dropped to the floor with a strangled cry. Stan didn't wait for a *thank you*. Bent to grab his leg. "Son of a bitch!"

It was shattered and useless.

He grabbed the handles of the cases. Pulled them off the tables to get going. Shrugged as he dropped the gun in favor of balance. One case in each hand. He was only three hops toward the stairs before realizing how much it was going to suck.

At the top of the stairs, he stopped to catch his breath. Spots in front of his eyes as he balanced on one shaky leg. Down the hall and into the front where the few employees pressed against the glass staring out into the dust hanging in the air. A man with his tie hanging over his shoulder — like he had moved so fast, it had flown behind him like a streamer — turned and spotted Stan and pointed with a dramatic gasp.

Stan heard a record scratch in his head, like he was the butt of a joke in a teenage comedy.

He hopped like an asshole toward the front doors, and the crowd parted to let him pass. Then he saw the four men closing in from outside. Goons in reserve.

Even if he knew where another exit was, he had no chance of getting there in time.

Their guns were drawn. Grim expression. Then blood exploded from the lead man's chest a split second before Stan heard the shot. The glass in the door shattered. More screaming behind him, but Stan stayed put. He didn't want to introduce any visual chaos that might hinder Haggis' shot.

The three remaining guys looked around in fear and confusion. Then the man closest to the bank lost most of his face. *Crack!*

The third man went down holding the bloody wound that magically appeared in his belly. *Pow!*

The last man stepped back with his face filling with dawning horror. He lifted his gun to point at Stan, and the left side of his head blew out. *Boom!* His body tried to keep him on his feet for a few steps, then he dropped to land face down.

Stan looked at all the glass and blood. Took a deep

breath and started hopping. Halfway through the door, he slipped and fell on his ass. Teeth snapped together, and a spasm in his lower back took his breath away. He held the cases to his chest and slid awkwardly on his right hip until he was clear of the mess, choking on the haze in the air.

Distant screams. Sirens and horns. Feet pounding on pavement, but when he looked they were going the other way. He made it to the corner by the alley. Almost got run over as he tried to stand. A Mercedes flew into the alley. A flash of the driver's angry face, and then the car screeched to a halt. The car backed out to run into a red pickup with the same idea.

Stan turned into the alley and laughed. The blue dumpsters were now blocking the way. Nobody was going down there, unless they wanted to get out and start pushing.

It was slow going. Leaning on the wall between hops. Lungs burning, back in agony, blood dripping off his jaw to soak his collar. When he got to the back corner, he finally saw the Subaru and Mo in the front seat. Gen behind him waving her hands frantically, pointing to where he stood.

When he saw it lurch forward, he knew he was going to be okay. Then he slid down to sit in the dirt as he waited.

Chapter Twenty-Three

Sitting in the Subaru behind the bank, Mo was as shocked as everybody else when he heard the explosion.

"Holy shit!" Gen shouted. "How much did you use?"

"Enough."

Then he heard the pop of Ian's thermos bomb. That was more like it. He shrugged with a sheepish smile. Pointed to the exterior lights on the bank. "It couldn't have been that bad. It was just loud."

"I felt it in my chest."

"Okay, okay, I get it. It may have been a little big, but everything's fine, right?"

"How do I know?"

He pressed himself into the seat. As a cloud of dust and smoke drifted by, he slouched a little lower. Gen pressed her face to the glass. "Did you bring the whole building down?"

"No ... just the second floor."

"Moses!"

"What? They wanted distraction. I know I'm distracted."

She burst out laughing. "Oh, calm down."

"I am calm."

"Then stop whining."

"I'm not fucking whining."

He felt her hand on his shoulder. "Oh my God. I'm just kidding."

He closed his eyes. "I know. Can we just drop it?"

Before she could answer, a car rocketed by, laying on the horn. He jumped in surprise, and Gen threw herself back with a squeaked, "Oh no!"

He sent a mean stare after the car that he knew the driver couldn't see.

Gen pointed to the bank. "The dumpsters."

He shrugged. "Yeah, so?"

"We need to move them into the alley. I was going to push them with the car, but I was worried about getting in the back so you could drive home 'cuz I can't do things without you making sure I'm doing them right."

The venom in her tone caught him off guard. He couldn't see her face leaning out of the rearview mirror's view.

He tried turning, but the car was too small. He grunted through his struggle and finally growled in frustration and jumped out of the car. Before he could close the door, she was out of the backseat.

He tried to grab her, but she stomped away. "What are you doing? What did that shit mean?"

She turned until she was walking backward. "Why don't you tell me what I mean, Mo?"

"What?" He stopped with his hands spread.

"I am a part of this. Jesus, how many times do we have to go over this? Are you really so insecure that you can't take a little joking criticism? Or that ..." She looked around like the word she was searching for would be hanging in the air. "Or believe I can do things for myself? Have you ever thought about what I did before we got together? Like I just walked around with a man in my pocket to jump out and throw his coat over every fucking puddle?"

The image of it popped into his mind, and he laughed before he could stop himself.

She ended at the dumpster. Putting her shoulder to the corner, she gave it a heave, and it moved with a grinding squeal of metal. She grunted and pushed again. Once there was room between the dumpster and the wall, she put her back to it. Pulled her feet up and pushed. As she straightened, the dumpster moved into the alley.

He had always been impressed by her strength and ability, but she rarely surprised him. He could only stare as she dropped down and dug her feet in to get the dumpster rolling on its tiny wheels.

He shook his head clear. Jogged over to put his shoulder into it next to her, and she elbowed him out of the way. "No! I can do it. *Without* you."

"But you don't have to."

"That's the fucking *point*! I don't need you to tell me how or why or when. Just trust in me. Know that I can and that I will. And then cheer me on. And if I fail, tell me it will be okay. Tell me to try again. Stop wrapping me in tissue paper."

She said the last sentence through tears. When he saw her reach for her braid and then collapse when it wasn't there, he wanted to pick her up and carry her away. Hold her until the dust cleared.

But he couldn't.

He held his hands up and nodded as he walked back to the car. By the time he sat back inside, she was attacking the dumpster again. Moving it by grudging inches. When she finally got it blocking the rest of the alley, she leaned against it with her head down. He could see her chest expanding in exhausted breaths.

He recognized the crack of a shot. Leaned out to tell her to get back to the car, but she was already moving. Walking with her head down and her hands on her hips.

Another shot, but she seemed not to notice. Then two more, and she slid into the backseat.

A car skidded to a screeching halt in the blocked alley. Honked and backed out with the engine revving.

Mo ignored it to look at her in the mirror. "Good job, babe," he said.

She smiled. Shook her head as she leaned back. Then she threw herself forward with a gasp. Both hands up and pointing like a spastic scarecrow pointing the way to Oz.

He turned just in time to see Stan slide down the corner. Blood covering his face. Suit jacket glistening and shiny. Hands streaked and dripping.

Mo jumped out with Gen on his heels, only beating her there because she was winded from pushing a ton of steel.

He didn't bother asking any questions. He just got Stan up and on his good foot. Held most of his weight across his shoulders. Gen grabbed the two cases. He knew her grip would have no problem with the wet handles.

Back to the Subaru, and when he dropped Stan in the passenger seat, he grabbed Mo's shirt. "They knew," he said.

"Who knew what?"

"They knew I was coming. Waited until I got there. What would you do if you knew where an enemy was going?"

Mo pulled Stan's hands away. "I'd ambush them."

"Yeah but what else?" Stan shouted as Mo closed the door and ran around to the other side. He dropped into the seat and fired the Subaru up. Its little engine sounded like a buzzing lawnmower.

"What *else?*" Stan cried again.

Mo squealed the small tires as he pulled away. Kept it in control as the rear end slipped back and forth. "I don't know, man. You tell *me.*"

Stan grabbed his arm and pulled himself across the space between seats. "I'd attack their base!"

Mo's foot slipped off the pedal as he finally understood what Stan was saying. He looked into Stan's desperate gaze.

"Oh no," Gen whispered.

Mo went as fast as the car would go. Even getting to speeds he never would have believed the car was capable of, it still felt like they were crawling along. By the look on Stan's face, he believed it was already too late.

When he looked up and saw Gen staring back, guilt filled him with nausea. He remembered yelling at Stan for being selfish for keeping his woman back at the motel. Where it was safe.

Chapter Twenty-Four

Ronnie jumped when a shape walked past the window. Just a shadow behind the curtains. Was it Stan already?

Maybe she should stand up for a while. She'd sat so long her ass was going numb.

A loud bang made her start so hard she slipped off the edge of the bed. She barely caught herself from crashing to the floor. The sound repeated, and the walls shook. Shouting from the room next door. Like there was a fight, but nobody was there. It was Gen and Mo's room. Did they come back early? Did something go wrong?

She got to her feet to run to the door, and just when she opened it, her mind screamed at her. She was making a huge mistake.

Two strangers came out of the room next door. Angry and red-faced. Shaking their heads. The one in front looked up and met her gaze. Stopped in his tracks so the second guy ran into him with a shout of frustration.

She threw herself back into the room. Swung the door toward the jamb, but a body stopped it cold. A hand crawling to the edge. Another hand with a gun in it.

The door tore from her grip, and the two men tumbled in.

She turned to run, even though there was nowhere to go, and there was sudden resistance from her shirt. Choking her and tearing at the throat as she was dragged back toward the door.

Instead of struggling to get away, she threw herself back, and they all fell in a struggling and cursing pile in the doorway. She reached behind her and grabbed whatever was under her fingers. Squeezing with everything she had. One hand was apparently holding something tougher than she wanted. The other one scored when she heard a strangled howl. Then she got her feet under her and turned to climb over them.

A hand shot up and grabbed the front of her waistband. Another one held onto her ankle. Pressure against the belly made her tip back. She couldn't step back to catch herself, and she went down to land flat on her back.

Breath whooshed out as her head cracked off the floor.

A bright light formed in her eyes as she turned to get a breath, but no air would come. Just a wheezing moan that sounded like winter wind through a loose window.

She managed to get to her knees where she straightened up and finally got her lungs to work, pulling in a rough breath that barely filled her up.

Pain exploded in her side, and she was struggling again, curled up on her side. One of them stood over her, pulling his foot back again. His toe dug into her hamstring. Her scream brought in air, but he kicked again. His foot made it through her guard, smashing into her fingers and burying into her stomach.

Fighting for air again when one of them said, "Don't kill her!"

She wanted to agree, and apparently the other one agreed because there were no other kicks. She could relax and try to breathe. They moved through the room. Checked the bathroom and the small kitchenette.

By the time they came back to her, she was breathing better, but she still kept herself in the fetal position. They weren't having it.

"Get up, bitch!"

Lifted by her hair, and the pain was exquisite, filling her whole mind with light. Then an arm around her throat, lifting her to her feet. Pressed into the bottom of her TFO, and the edge bit into her chin. The delicate new skin around her mouth. Cutting up into the bottom of what little nose she had.

The pressure released when the guy holding her up hissed in pain. "This fucking thing," he said.

She didn't want to know what thing he was talking about, but he answered her by ripping her mask off. She felt blood flowing down her face, and she sagged into him. Why make a bad thing worse? Not killing her didn't matter anymore.

She remembered Stan saying they would use her against him. Hold her so he would do what they wanted. And there it was. They were going to hurt her to hurt him.

As they dragged her out the door, they delivered slaps. More choking. Yanking and pulling on her hair. She wanted to tell them she wasn't going to fight. They could do whatever they wanted and she wouldn't even make a sound.

If she had kept pushing like Gen had, she would be with them now. Then she thought about Shawna. Mohammed and Jeanette.

She heard pops. Like gunfire. Or firecrackers.

"Get some," one of her kidnappers said.

She didn't know what the *some* was, but the gunshots stopped. Out in the parking lot, and she looked up to see the black Dodge Charger parked in a spot in the middle. Nothing on either side like it carried an evil that repelled other cars.

A few steps from it, and she felt like she was flying. Spinning in the air. She hit the front fender with her hip. Folded onto it, and her forehead bounced off the hood. She slid down the side in daze, but arms slipped under her arms. Fingers dug into her breasts as he pulled her back to her feet and slung her toward the rear. A hand on her head pushed her down. Pushed her into the backseat, and he got in next to her. The other door opened, and before she could try to crawl toward it, it filled with the body of the other man. As he got in to sit down, he sat her up by pulling on her hair again.

She clamped her teeth on the scream. She decided not to make a sound. Let them do their worst. She wouldn't give them what they wanted.

They pressed in against her. The heat was already stifling. Her ribs hurt, and she still couldn't get a full breath. Blood and sweat trickled down her face. The cuts in the skin around her mouth stung like bands of ice.

She looked down at her hands. One of the nails had torn off, leaving a bed of raw hamburger.

"Did you fucking hear me, bitch?" the thug on the right asaid.

She actually hadn't, but she wasn't going to argue. He raised his fist and brought it down on her thigh.

Her foot kicked out on reflex, and her quad muscles began to twitch. She grabbed it with both hands curled over it as the pain ran down into her knee.

A hand on the back of her head, and she braced for more hair pulling, pushing back to help him pull her up so it wouldn't hurt so bad.

When she opened her eyes, she saw a white van creep by. Just like the one that was in the lot earlier in the morning. Then she saw the driver as he turned his head to look directly into her eyes before staring back out the front.

Or the van looked like Ian's because *that's* who was driving it. She looked down and smiled.

"What's so fucking funny?" Left Thug demanded.

She folded her hands in her lap. "I promised myself I wasn't going to tell you two shit."

Her throat hurt, and her voice sounded like it had when it was still burned. Two steps forward, one step back ...

"Oh, you're gonna fucking talk, bitch," Right Thug said.

"That's what I mean," Ronnie told him. "I *wasn't* going to talk, but now I am."

She saw Ian walking toward her. Dropped each hand onto a thigh for a soft caress. "If you'll stop hurting me ... I'll talk."

Left Thug slipped his hand away, but Right Thug pulled it up to sit it on his crotch. "That's more like it."

"Just tell us where Stan Manning is. We've lost contact with the bank."

"Don't tell her that," Right Thug hissed.

"It's okay," Ronnie said. "I'm not going to tell you that. But I will tell you this."

Left Thug crossed his arms. "And what's that?"

She dug her hand into Right Thug's balls. Swung her elbow up into Left Thug's face.

"Fuck you! *That's* what I'm gonna tell you!"

Right Thug's knees came up to try to protect his balls. Left Thug jerked to the side with a grunt of pain. Threw an elbow of his own. The sound of it hitting her forehead was like gunfire and shattering glass. Eyes full of light, then blackness spread across her vision as she slumped forward.

Chapter Twenty-Five

As Ian neared Stan's motel, he calmed down. A bleak dread slowing his mind. It was where they were all going to meet before splitting up the copies, setting the spam servers off, and going the way of the wind.

If she was still alive, that's where she would be. If she was dead, then he was delaying it. He didn't have to see it yet. Therefore it hadn't happened. It wasn't real.

He pulled into a spot facing the door to Stan's room. It was hanging open. The room looked empty. Next to it was the other room. Also open, but the jamb showed signs of forced entry. Cracked wood and shattered trim hanging at an angle.

He reached behind him to pull the laptop back up on the center console. Started the snooper and scanned for radio signals. Filtered out all the Wi-Fi and radio. Focused on com bursts, like a person checking in to a number that wasn't answering.

Found one coming from nearby, right in the parking lot. He looked out the window, and snorted bitter laughter.

Of course. He could have just looked. Saved the trouble of a search.

He threw the laptop in the back. Pulled out to drive up to the Charger just using the idle power of the motor and moving at a crawl. Nobody was in the front seat.

Then he got to the front and could see into the back. The silhouette of Ronnie's hair between two large shadows. He looked at where he thought her eyes would be. Willed her to see him, Then he faced front and drove to the edge of the lot. Parked in a strip of gravel so the van faced the other entrance. At last he wouldn't have to bust a fence down.

He grabbed his hardhat. That plus his vest gave him a bit of visual authority. He looked like an official something. Sometimes something small like that could get people to listen to you. Just act like you know what's up.

He got out, leaving the van running. Walked like he was doing a study of the cracking asphalt. Looked up at the Dodge as he neared. Saw it rocking, like somebody was jumping around inside. Then it really got to moving. So maybe a *few* someones.

He continued with his head down like he was still doing his parking lot audit. Glanced up to see them struggling in the backseat. One face twisted in pain. Then an elbow coming up to crash into Ronnie's head. When she slumped forward, he had his chance.

He drew and fired through the window. Glass exploded inward, and the man grimacing in pain didn't have much of a mouth left to grimace with anymore. A few quick steps, and Ian was reaching past the man's shattered jaw to put two in his temple. Then he drew back and put a final shot in the first man's face.

Holstered his pistol and opened the door. Ignored the voices of people coming out their doors and gathering into groups of gawkers. They pointed at him as he bent into the car. He dragged the guy out to splat on the pavement. Then pulled Ronnie across the seat. Her head lolled, then snapped upright. She gasped and tried to fight his hands. "It's all right," he said. "It's me, it's *me*."

He couldn't think of anything else, but it didn't matter. At the sound of his voice, she calmed. Leaned into him as he pulled her to her feet and followed along beside him.

Instead of running straight to his van, he walked toward the growing crowd. At the sight of shattered glass falling from her hair and sticking to her bloody face — and the scars underneath looking like she had run face first into the sun — they shied away.

"Somebody call the police," he shouted. "They tried to kill her, and then they shot each other."

He swung her around and headed toward the end of the lot. "She needs a doctor. I'm taking her to a hospital. Get out of the way. Call the police!"

All the cops were a little busy, but they didn't need to know that. They just needed conflicting evidence. Somebody saw him shoot the men in the Dodge. Some heard that the men had shot each other. Just a little more confusion to add to what had happened in Old Downtown.

He helped her into the van. Ran around to the other side. Made sure he didn't spin gravel out at the bystanders as he pulled away.

He turned away from the motel, even though he was screaming at himself to go right there. He didn't want the people behind him watching him drive right across the street.

So a slow circuit around the block. Then pulling in from the other side to see a crowd in front of his door. People looking at all the blood he could see from his vantage point sitting so high up.

The bodies on the floor. Piled in the doorway. The brown uniforms of a Household Services contractor. More than his two team members. The body all the way in the back by the table. A gory spread of blood on the wall.

The color drained from his life. The only sound came from inside the van. Mostly his own desperate breath. "She's gone," he said.

He turned to face the windshield. Drove through the parking lot to head east. "Now how am I going to tell her?"

"I'm so sorry," Ronnie said.

He thought he was going to be okay until that moment. Her words cut through his restraint, and he burst into tears. He pulled to the side of the road. A horn blared as a speeding truck passed. He dropped his head into his hands and wept.

When she climbed up over the center console to drape herself over him in sympathy he turned to hold her against him in an awkward embrace. "There's no light left," he wailed. "Why is it so dark?"

He didn't know how long he sat there. She never rushed him. Never complained. Just let him get it out, and when it was, he was empty.

No color. No light. No feelings.

He wiped his face and pulled back onto the highway. "Thank you," he whispered.

She didn't say anything. Like she knew he wanted to be silent. Just the sound of the road as he left the only thing he had ever loved behind him.

Chapter Twenty-Six

Mo had to take it a little easier. He almost got lost on the way back. "That's what happened to me," Gen shouted.

He ignored her until he got his bearings back. "See?"

"Just fucking get there," Stan said. His face was ghastly under the blood. Gray around his eyes. Sweaty. He breathed like he was having a heart attack.

Then he turned and fixed him with a critical stare. "What was with the explosion? Trying to get to the moon?"

Mo felt his irritation rise. Bit it back. "It got the job done."

Stan nodded. "It got *all* the jobs done."

Everybody fell silent as they continued to the motel. Slowing for the ambulance. Twice for a fire engine. Another two times for cops.

They pulled in to see people milling around in front of the doors. Their rooms. Mo slowed down as they pulled even, but Stan slouched down. "Keep going."

"What? We have to see."

"Keep fucking going. They're turning to look, for fuck's sake. Go like nothing is wrong."

"But something *is* wrong," Gen shouted.

"Shut the fuck up," Stan hissed.

Mo agreed, but he would liked to have it framed differently. He drove without looking at the crowds. Like he was planning on driving through anyway. Then he slowed again at the Charger. "Motherfucker."

Rear windows blown out. A body in the parking lot. Another slouched inside.

"The fuck are we driving into?"

"What happened?" Gen said.

Stan put his face in his hands. "They beat us. I told you. They were *here*. They knew the whole time."

"Yeah, but we got the evidence."

"I don't care about the evidence. They have *Ronnie*."

"How do you know?"

"I saw her mask on the floor when we drove by the room."

Gen grabbed a double handful of her hair. "No!"

Mo shook his head. "But what about the Dodge? All shot up like that. Who did *that*?"

"Ooh, maybe it was Ian," Gen said. "He came back and caught them trying to take her. Maybe he *saved* her."

Stan dropped his hands in his lap. "Maybe."

Mo tipped his head in thought. "I bet that's it."

"Then let's get across the street."

Gen leaned forward. "There's a lot of people over there too."

Mo didn't bother hiding his intentions; he went straight across. Rolled by as the inside of the car got quieter the closer they got to the crowd standing outside Ian's door.

"Look at the blood," Gen whispered.

Mo took a single glance. Kept going like he didn't see shit. "We check out Haggis' room too?"

Stan shook his head. "His truck is still here."

Gen shook her head. "Maybe he's just not back yet."

"Maybe."

"We can't just go by without checking. Jeanette might be in there."

"Or somebody might be waiting. Plus, do you have a key to the door?"

Mo sighed. "No, but I can get in."

"Fine. Park and check it out, but I can't go. I'm a little *conspicuous*, what with the blood and one foot."

Mo pulled in right in front. So much attention was focused on the other end, nobody looked his way. "Come on, girl. And bring my bag."

She jumped out and followed him to the door. Handed him the backpack and stood to block the view from the people gathering to look at the massacre.

He slid his lock pick gun out. Worked the lock like he had the one at the surplus store. "If this had been those electronic shits, I wouldn't have had a chance."

Right when he got the lock to turn and was pushing into the room, Gen said, "Should we have knocked first?"

He got an image of Jeanette Gustoff running up on him with a gun, but it was dark inside. Nobody there.

He shrugged. "She ain't home, so it doesn't matter."

Gen pointed to the bed. "Look. She was packed. So where is she?"

"Grab it."

"What?"

"If we find her, we give her the bag back. If we don't, I don't think she'll care."

She nodded, and he suddenly missed how her braid would bounce when she did that. She bounced over to grab the bag. Ran outside, and he closed the door to follow her. It didn't latch, but he didn't care. Still nobody paying attention.

When he got back behind the wheel, he paused to put his hand on Stan's arm. "If they want her to get to you, she's alive."

Stan nodded. "I know. But what are they doing to her?"

"Maybe nothing."

Stan shook as he cried. Held his hands over his mouth. "They're rapists. Abusing and killing little girls. My cousin. A fucking senator. They'll just hang on to her and play fucking cribbage? They're fucking animals, and they've *got* her!"

Mo looked back at Gen. Knew he would be just as desperate and anguished if it was her.

He drove to the exit and paused before turning. "Where are we going? The park?"

Stan took so long to answer, Mo thought he had fallen asleep. "Yeah. Back to the park. We'll find my fiancée. And kill whoever hurt her."

Mo smiled his approval. "My man."

Chapter Twenty-Seven

Haggis grinned as he packed up. What a fucking explosion. Exhilarating. And the shots he took? Through heavy debris. Blowing tree limbs. An extreme angle.

Maybe only a hundred guys in the world could have made those shots.

A nice slow pack-up. Taking his time with the old girl. If he never used her again, it would be okay. A guy could get used to a little peace and quiet.

He threw his pack on his shoulder, and before he left the alcove, he dug in his pocket. Took the twenty dollar bill back out. Dropped it into the corner. If somebody ever crawled in here for shelter, he hoped they'd find it.

When he got to the bottom level, he thought about just walking. It wasn't too far, and the day was turning out to be bright and beautiful. The breeze blowing the dust and smoke toward the bank so it wouldn't be in his face on the way home.

He decided against it when he realized he needed to get back sooner rather than later so he could hear the story of why Stan came out of the bank looking like he just lost a prize fight, hopping on one foot to the alley.

Haggis slapped himself on the thigh. Then Stan had almost been run over by that Mercedes.

Haggis stopped laughing as he climbed into the SUV. Tossed his pack in the passenger seat. Started her up and put her in gear. Pulled out his phone before driving out and dialed the room.

When there was no answer, he felt a twinge of worry. But maybe she was in the shower. He sped up when he called again, and there was still no answer.

By the time he got to the roundabout in the center of town, he was driving faster than was probably prudent under the circumstances, but when the cops buzzed by going the other way after the second ambulance or so, he felt confident in kicking her up a little.

He saw the crowd before he rounded the bushes at the end of the parking lot. He pulled the SUV into an empty spot, crooked as shit, and left it running to get out and jog to the door.

It was a bloodbath inside. But only five bodies. He tried to look into every part of the room without going inside or pushing anybody out of the way.

Where was she? What had happened?

He recognized Shawna and Mohammed. Didn't know the other three, but they were dressed the same. The same uniforms all around.

He never got that. Like they were a guild or something. Like the freemasons.

He bit his lip to keep from crying as he turned to scan the parking lot.

"Hey, you hear what happened?" a voice sounded behind him, pinched and whiny.

He shook his head. "No. Just an explosion and a couple of shots."

"An explosion?" He focused on who was speaking. A thin woman with a cigarette clamped between her stained lips. "Here?"

"Oh, I thought you meant back *there*."

"Back there *where*?"

He didn't answer. Instead, he walked down to the end of the rooms. Maybe she was still inside. He had his key out before he got there, but when he put it in, the door opened. Her bag was gone.

He spun around. Maybe it was in the truck. That's where he had put all his things. Just the old girl.

He cursed himself. His rifle was in the SUV, which was just sitting there running and unlocked.

Losing the two greatest ladies in his life at the same time?

He jogged back to the SUV, and she was still there. He reached in and slung her over his shoulder. Took her to his truck, but Jeanette wasn't in it. He hung his head and unlocked the passenger door.

He had given Jeanette a spare key. Just in case she needed to go get a coffee or just wait for him inside. If she wasn't here … did they have her?

Where would he go? How would he find her? If Ian's team was dead, did he know? Was he dead too? Had anybody made it out?

He dropped his pack on the seat and ran around to climb in. He would go to the park like they had agreed. If he was the only one there, he would take it from there.

As he pulled through the parking lot, he looked over at his backpack. He steered the truck to the side.

"That's *her* seat," he said. Hardly enough time sitting

there to make it a habit or ritual, but she would slide over and hug up on him and put her hand on his thigh.

He shook his head in apology to the old girl in the backpack. "It's *Jeanette's* seat."

He got out, sliding the bag across the seat. Pulled his keys to run to the back and unlock the cover. He froze when he saw blood on the bumper. Looked around, but saw nothing but the crowd still focused on the carnage inside.

Another speck of blood on top of the tailgate. He unlocked it, lowered it down, and almost dropped the old girl when he saw the new one curled up in the bed.

He didn't know what to do. Couldn't figure out how she had closed it behind her. Or even how she had gotten in there in the first place.

He slid the backpack in next to her and reached for her leg. There was so much blood.

When she moaned, he gasped in relief. Jumped in to gently ease her out. She grunted in pain, and he cradled her. Backed up. Lifted a boot to kick the tailgate closed. Felt like a muscle in his groin was trying to rip off his pelvis, but he got it. Ran her to the front, easing up when she cried out.

Got the door open and slid her in. "It's okay," he said.

"I'm not so sure," she replied, and his knees almost dropped him to the ground. He shut the door. Ran around the front, holding the pain in his groin with a digging fist. He should have left the tailgate open. Closed it while running around the back, but it was too late. He'd just have to deal with it. At least he hadn't been injured like her.

He got in and leaned over her. "I'll take you to the hospital."

"No."

"You've been *shot*."

"Take me to the park. To where they are waiting."

"Jeanette, honey. You're *hurt*."

"The evidence is all in the back of the truck. I got it before … I got it."

Her voice faded.

His vision blurred as he bent back over her, but he felt her breath warm against his cheek. He kissed her forehead and sat back up. "Okay."

He drove away, taking the evidence to the park. Maybe somebody would be there to take it. Maybe she would survive the trip. Maybe …

He couldn't stop looking at her.

Maybe she was dying.

If it saved those little girls, she would think it was worth it. He wasn't sure if he ever would.

Chapter Twenty-Eight

Stan wondered how it had gone so bad. Was it his fault? Ian's? Could anybody be blamed?

The Subaru bounced over the rocks as Mo pulled into the park. Around the bend past a stand of decorative grass. When they emerged to see the gazebo they had slept at when they first got to Belling, he saw Ian's van.

He nearly broke into fresh tears. Somebody else had made it.

When he saw Ronnie's fuzzy head, he lost control. The sobbing he had held at bay broke through his resolve, and he became a broken, weeping mess.

He tried getting out before Mo stopped. Stepped out with his missing right leg to plunge to the ground. Landed on his face to grind his cheek into the dirt. Rolled over to see her standing over him. Her face torn and bruised and scarred and absolutely gorgeous.

She fell into his arms, and he held her.

After crying into each other's shoulders for several minutes — murmured words and reassurances — she finally stood up. He tried to get up to join her, but Mo was there to help. Stood him up and helped him to the table where Ian sat with Gen.

She held his hand, but he didn't seem to notice. His face was a blank of hanging skin.

When Stan got settled, Ronnie sat next to him. Burrowed against him like she couldn't get close enough. Like she wanted to share the same space.

Ian glanced over at her, and his eyes softened. A ghost of a smile. Then it disappeared when he faced Stan. Back to the hollowed-eye stare of a haunted man.

It was clear that Ian blamed himself.

"I'm sorry about your team," Stan said.

Ian nodded his head once. "Thank you." Then he looked at Gen's hand. Pulled his away and looked at her. "There's a first-aid kit in the van. It's very nicely appointed. I can call and have some blood here, but otherwise, I think it will work. Can you get it please?"

Gen nodded, but before she could stand, Ian leaned toward her and took her hand. "Thank you." He didn't seem to realize tears were streaming down his face. He looked at Ronnie. "Thank *you*."

Stan was amazed at seeing this man cry. He had seen more emotion from him during this mission than at any other time during their association, but crying … it was like hearing Eeyore laugh.

Ian nodded as he pulled his hand into his lap and watched Gen walk to the van.

Ronnie kissed Stan on the shoulder and got up to follow her friend. Even Mo left him to face Ian alone. He didn't know what to do.

"It was my fault," he whispered. "All my fault."

Stan shook his head and started to argue, but Ian looked up with his dead eyes, and Stan clamped his mouth shut.

"They killed them."

Stan shook his head. "Who?"

"My team killed them. They did their job."

Stan had to look away. "I got the evidence."

"That's good. I'll take it."

"How's that?"

Ian took a deep breath, like he was trying to calm himself. "I will take it. All of it."

"Why?"

"Because I will finish the job."

"But I haven't paid you."

Ian pursed his lips. "I will finish the job. You will disappear. We will never see each other again."

Stan wasn't sure what was happening. "How will I pay you?"

"We will never see each other again."

Stan spread his hands. "I can't … Ian. I will not let you go knowing I owe you so much. You deserve to get paid."

"No. I'm an independent contractor now. I decide my own fee, and I have decided on zero."

"Ian, I have a million dollars in a case in the —"

"Use it to hide then!"

Stan sighed in frustration. Ian smiled, and it was more disturbing than the tears. "Your lady held me when I needed to cry. The way my mother did when I was a boy. And it was the first time I had ever remembered her in a positive way. She was evil. But when I was small, before she started hurting me, she loved me. Ronnie is special. Then Gen told me something about Shawna I did not know. It has filled me with …" He looked up like he was searching for the word. "A lightness. Like the fluff on top of a pie."

"Meringue."

His face brightened. And he grinned. It looked like the leer of a skull. "Yes. Like *that*. She told me that Shawna wanted me. *Me*! Can you believe that? What a lucky man I would have been. Which is why it twisted in my heart to hear it. You see, Stan. I was afraid to tell her. And now she's gone. But I'm not afraid anymore."

Stan didn't know what else to say. "That's good, Ian. I'm glad that you're no longer afraid."

Ian's smile became wistful. Then it faded, and his eyes become hollow again. He looked like a doll somebody had thrown to the side of the road. "I have nothing left. You have a life still. Ronnie and your friends. You take your money and hide. Protect them and yourself. And have … something I wish I had done more of. Have fun. Love each other. And tell each other."

"What are you going to do?"

"I'm going to burn it down. Then I'll find another one. Burn it down too. Until I have killed enough of them to equal one of her."

He looked up like something caught his attention. Stan turned his head to listen. When he heard tires on gravel, he spun around. Nearly fell off his seat when his other leg wasn't there to brace.

Gen walked by with a giant white case on wheels. A handle extended so she could pull it along behind her. "It has a fucking defibrillator in it," she said. When she saw his face, her eyes widened, and she spun to look.

It was Haggis' truck. Stan's face burned when he realized he hadn't even asked about him since seeing Jeanette's room empty. When he saw nobody in the passenger seat, he closed his eyes. Another one gone. Sad to see. Relief because it wasn't Ronnie. Then guilt.

He lowered his head into his hands. He heard the door open. Haggis' feet hit the dirt. Then his voice. "I think she's dying."

When he heard Jeanette's voice, Stan's eyes sprang open.

"I'm *not* dying. I just kinda wish I was."

Gen jumped to help Haggis get her out of the truck.

"She needs a hospital," Haggis said.

"I don't. The bleeding's stopped. I just need some whiskey and a good night's sleep. And a shower."

By the sound of her voice, she needed more than that. It had no substance, like she was barely there.

Stan wanted to get up and help. He didn't even have his crutch, and if he tried hopping again, his knee would give out. His back was still screaming.

"We can't stay here," Ian said.

At the sound of his voice, they all stopped. He stood up and walked to Jeanette. "How did you get injured?"

Haggis stepped in between them. "She's tired right now. She needs to —"

Ian moved like a light turning on. A blink of motion, and a gun barrel sank into Haggis' belly.

"Whoa!" Mo shouted as Gen dropped the handle of the giant first-aid kit.

"What are you doing?" she cried.

Ian ignored them and held Haggis' gaze. "How did you get injured?" he repeated.

Jeanette pushed out of Gen's support and edged past Haggis with a wince of pain. Her face looked like an eggshell, waxy and pale. "They fought for me," she said. Stan had to strain to hear her. "First Jihad. Then Shawna. She stood in front of me. Shielded me. And the last one shot her." She hitched in a breath as tears poured from her eyes. "And then I shot *him*."

Ian nodded. "And the evidence?"

"It's all in the back of the truck."

With the same speed, the gun was gone, and Ian was walking away. Stan blinked like he had missed something.

They watched him lean into the back of the truck, come back out with an arm of bloody folders, and latch the tailgate before going to the Subaru.

"It's the one on the right," Mo shouted.

Ian reached in and grabbed the case, unlatched it, and looked inside. When he closed it and stood back up, he looked at Stan. "You have to leave here. Get up to Austin. A motel on the edge of town out by the airport in all those bushes. Hole up there for two weeks. Move to another place. Another two weeks. Lay low. Don't be stupid. And when you hear it on the news, then you *really* run."

He climbed into the van and drove away.

They stood in silence until the sound of the van was lost in the distance.

"I'd really like that whiskey now," Jeanette said.

When she passed out, Haggis was there to catch her.

Chapter Twenty-Nine

Haggis looked out at the ocean. He'd never been to Mexico. Germany, the Middle East, Africa, all over the United States. But not down south of the border.

Clear water and white sand. On a resort well away from the kids partying night and day.

He and Jeanette had been living in a cabin in Etowa, Tennessee when the news broke. On a hill overlooking a line of trees above the interstate. Puttering around the property. Exploring each other's bodies. Taking care of scars. Physical and emotional.

For the first time in decades, Haggis had settled into the notion that he no longer needed to move on. Then he had gotten Stan's letter. Ten thousand dollars, a brochure for a private resort in Riviera Maya, and a date. Even then, he wasn't in a hurry to move on.

When Jeanette had seen it, she had shrugged before dropping it back on the counter. Then she said what he had been thinking. "I wonder how he knew where we were."

Haggis laughed. "Maybe we should go then. A guy could ask him."

She walked over with her glass of wine and sat in his lap. "A gal wouldn't mind, I guess."

The story became a global fascination. In constant rotation on every channel. Thousands of LiveLyfe videos. Spam in hundreds of millions of inboxes.

Not since the MeToo movement had there been this level of retribution. Families coming forward. Informants spilling their guts. Political parties scrambling to be the most apologetic, promising to get to the bottom of the sweeping allegations.

Proving that votes were more important than children. Done in the name of the very same children that were being mourned worldwide.

He took a pull from the straw rising out of his frozen margarita and leaned back as the breeze blew past the posts that held up the roof on his private cabana. The last in a line of ten, connected by a weathered pier. Right over the water.

He turned from the view of the bright horizon and looked back at the beach. The smiling Mexican that had brought his drink was almost back up to the gate that led into the rest of the resort. Waving at the other guests and pausing to take more orders.

The wedding had been done for more than four hours, and he had just wanted a moment to himself. He knew there was going to be a party, and he was ready ... he just wanted a breath.

Stan and Ronnie had worn white. Stan almost as tan as Ronnie's natural color. Mo and Gen had been dressed like typical tourists. Gen's only concession being a long veil, her belly heavy with their little girl.

Stan had asked if Haggis and Jeanette wanted to take

advantage of the opportunity, but Haggis had declined. They had been married for three months already.

Stan still had the video. It didn't seem like it had any value anymore since the whole world had seen it, but maybe he was just superstitious.

No word from Ian, except for the results of his efforts blowing the story up, and Haggis couldn't help wanting to see him again. The man had been hurting the last time he had seen him. It was a shame to be in so much pain with nobody by your side to help ease it.

Ronnie, Gen, and Jeanette were in a circle. Holding hands and dancing on the sand. He had a hard time with the guilt sometimes. Benefitting from a tragedy. But he had seen her grow into happiness. His wife and his life, and he couldn't imagine existing without her.

Mo's wide grin when he looked at Gen mirrored his own, just like the way Stan's did.

Haggis finished his drink and stood up to carry the empty glass to the beach. He looked back at the ocean, closed his eyes against another salty breeze, and breathed it in.

This was for any child that had suffered. Died as a result of abuse. Or the ones that had survived with the memories.

He could tell himself he felt good about where he was, even though it was only possible because somebody else had suffered so much.

He left the cabana to join his friends. Yup. A guy was ready to stay put for the first time in his life.

～

IAN DIDN'T BOTHER DISGUISING his vehicle. He still

drove the standard white van that he was used to. It was comfortable and had the utility he needed.

But even after all this time he looked into the mirror, expecting to see her looking back at him.

It had taken him weeks to prepare the evidence for its public debut. In an apartment outside of Ybor City. Lots of Cuban food and cigars.

Poring over every detail. Arranging it into a concise flow. Hiding one person's involvement. Scrubbing a name from the files, like erasing somebody's identity.

A Russian firm had taken 13,000 dollars to set up the new servers he needed. He funded their efforts to spread disinformation on LiveLyfe in exchange for bandwidth. He had no worries that they were going to affect any actual change in America's political process because as soon as he scorched the Internet with his spam bomb, the feds would shut the servers down, and the Russians would be out of business.

Years of oversight committees would probably lead to meaningful oversight in how foreign entities were able to access domestic services.

Ian didn't care that it was a win for his nation. He just wanted to manipulate the system America's enemies used. Russia would do in a pinch, and since he was a solo operative now, he just happened to be in that pinch.

He wore the traditional brown of a Household Services contractor, but he had the unicorn hat on that Shawna had bought for him. Rumpled and stained with sweat, but he never went outside without it. It was hard to look official with it, but he had no cover to blow. He pulled it down lower over his eyes as he got out of the van.

The neighborhood was one of those designer communities. Private security — easily bribed as his 1,000 dollars to the roaming guards had proven — and unified lawn services. A tropical color palette the brochure said was tasteful. It was his experience that most rich people had no taste.

He had no props. Just a knife drawn from a sheath sitting inside his right cargo pocket. He didn't care if every house on the block was watching. He was just this task away from finishing the job.

He climbed the steps up to the front door. He noticed it opened to the right, so he shifted the knife to his left hand. He rang the doorbell, then knocked. Loosened his knees and tightened his grip.

The maid had taken the family Mercedes wagon to the grocery. The new wife was getting her toes done.

Ian heard the deadbolt disengage. The suck of air as the door opened.

Ty Kirby squinted out into the bright light of the Florida sun that had watched the soil get soaked in innocent blood from the Seminoles being chased by Andrew Jackson to a little girl raped and murdered and left in the mud of a swamp.

Ian didn't want to hear the man's voice, so he swung before the door was open enough for Kirby to see what was coming.

The blade pierced the skin under the right side of Kirby's stubbled jaw. Metal gleamed through his open mouth as the point jammed into the soft palate at the back of his throat.

Whatever he had been going to say was lost in his choking cry.

Ian had saved him from the resulting investigation by wiping his involvement in Pedophile Junction clean. He imagined Kirby had wondered at his luck. At seeing powerful men and women fall to the hammer of justice and public opinion. Never knowing that he was being saved for last.

Kirby stumbled back. Blood frothing from his lips. Eyes wide in horror and pain. The knife quivering as his mouth worked to make words.

Ian followed him inside and closed the door behind him. When he drew his pistol, Kirby's voice became a rising scream. His hand out in front of him.

Ian shot Kirby in the crotch. In the chest. In the head. When the body fell backward to land spread out on the polished foyer tile, Ian stepped up to stand over him. Fired into his face until the pistol was empty. Then he dropped it into the mess that had been Kirby's horrified expression.

He turned and let himself out.

A job well done.

Frank Grimm is a retired detective who breaks into his neighbors' homes searching for clues to find the man who murdered his daughter. But he soon finds another young girl who needs help.

Will Frank's rusty skills be enough to stop the killer before another girl dies?

Get Hidden Justice now!

A Quick Favor

Thanks for reading *Cold Retribution*.

If you enjoyed this book, please consider writing a review of it on your favorite bookselling site so other readers can enjoy it too. Just a couple of sentences would mean a lot to me.

Thank you!

Nolon & Dave

About the Authors

Nolon King writes fast-paced psychological thrillers set in the glitzy world of entertainment's power players with a bold, insightful voice. He's not afraid to explore the darker side of human nature through stories featuring families torn apart by secrets and lies.

Nolon loves to write about big questions and moral quandaries. How far would you go to cover up an honest mistake? Would you destroy your career to protect your family? How much of your soul would you sell to get the life of your dreams? Would you cheat on your husband to keep your children safe? Would you give in to a stalker's demands to save your marriage?

David W. Wright is the co-author of edge-of-your-seat thrillers including the best-selling post-apocalyptic series *Yesterday's Gone,* the paranoid sci-fi *WhiteSpace* series, and the vigilante series, *No Justice,* as well as standalone thrillers *12,* and *Crash* which was recently optioned for a movie.

David is an accomplished, though intermittent, cartoonist who lives in [LOCATION REDACTED] with his wife and son [NAMES REDACTED.]

He is not at all paranoid.

He is "the grumpy one" on *The Story Studio Podcast* with fellow Sterling and Stone founders, Sean Platt and Johnny B. Truant.

You can email him at <u>david@sterlingandstone.net</u>

We swear, he almost never bites. Unless you feed him after midnight.

Also By Nolon King

Cold Justice

Cold Justice

Cold Reckoning

Cold Retribution

Hidden Justice

Hidden Justice

Hidden Honor

Hidden Shame

Hidden Virtue

No Justice

No Justice

No Escape

No Hope

No Return

No Stopping

No Fear

Once Upon A Crime

Once Upon A Crime

Twice Upon A Lie

Three Times a Murder

Dead For Good

Dead For Good

Also By David W. Wright

Cold Justice

Cold Justice

Cold Reckoning

Cold Retribution

Hidden Justice

Hidden Justice

Hidden Honor

Hidden Shame

Hidden Virtue

No Justice

No Justice

No Escape

No Hope

No Return

No Stopping

No Fear

Karma Police

Jumper

Karma Police

The Collectors

Deviant

The Fall

Homecoming

Yesterday's Gone

October's Gone

Yesterday's Gone Season One

Yesterday's Gone Season Two

Yesterday's Gone Season Three

Yesterday's Gone Season Four

Yesterday's Gone Season Five

Yesterday's Gone Season Six

Tomorrow's Gone

Tomorrow's Gone Season One

Tomorrow's Gone Season Two

Tomorrow's Gone Season Three

Available Darkness

Darkness Itself

Available Darkness Book One

Available Darkness Book Two

Available Darkness Book Three

WhiteSpace

WhiteSpace Season One

WhiteSpace Season Two

WhiteSpace Season Three

Stand Alone Novels

12

Crash

Emily's List

Threshold